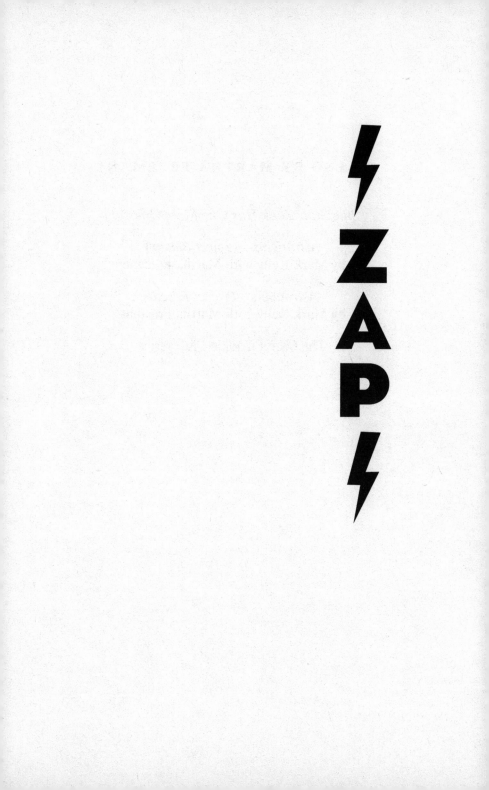

ZAP!

martha
freeman

A Paula Wiseman Book

Simon & Schuster Books for Young Readers
NEW YORK LONDON TORONTO SYDNEY NEW DELHI

SIMON & SCHUSTER BOOKS FOR YOUNG READERS
An imprint of Simon & Schuster Children's Publishing Division
1230 Avenue of the Americas, New York, New York 10020

SIMON & SCHUSTER BOOKS FOR YOUNG READERS
is a trademark of Simon & Schuster, Inc.
For information about special discounts for bulk purchases,
please contact Simon & Schuster Special Sales at 1-866-506-1949 or
business@simonandschuster.com.
The Simon & Schuster Speakers Bureau can bring authors to your live event.
For more information or to book an event,
contact the Simon & Schuster Speakers Bureau at 1-866-248-3049 or
visit our website at www.simonspeakers.com.
Jacket design by Krista Vossen
Interior design by Hilary Zarycky
The text for this book was set in Life.
Manufactured in the United States of America
1217 FFG
First Edition
2 4 6 8 10 9 7 5 3 1
Names: Freeman, Martha, 1956– author.|
Title: Zap! / Martha Freeman.
Description: First edition. | New York : Simon & Schuster Books for Young Readers, [2018] | "A Paula Wiseman Book." | Summary: Eleven-year-olds Luis and Maura investigate the cause of a long-term, citywide power outage in Hampton, New Jersey. Includes facts about electric power and instructions for assembling an emergency kit. | Includes bibliographical references.
Identifiers: LCCN 2017028131| ISBN 9781534405578 (hardcover) |
ISBN 9781534405592 (e-book)
Subjects: | CYAC: Electric power failures—Fiction. | Family life—New Jersey—Fiction. | Computer crimes—Fiction. | Hacking—Fiction. | Nicaraguan Americans—Fiction. | New Jersey—Fiction. | Mystery and detective stories.
Classification: LCC PZ7.F87496 Zap 2018 | DDC [Fic]—dc23
LC record available at https://lccn.loc.gov/2017028131

For my smart, generous, and fast friend,
Anthony H. LoCicero III,
who brought up the electric grid
one day over coffee.

We live in a society exquisitely dependent on science and technology, in which hardly anyone knows anything about science and technology. This is a clear prescription for disaster.

—CARL SAGAN

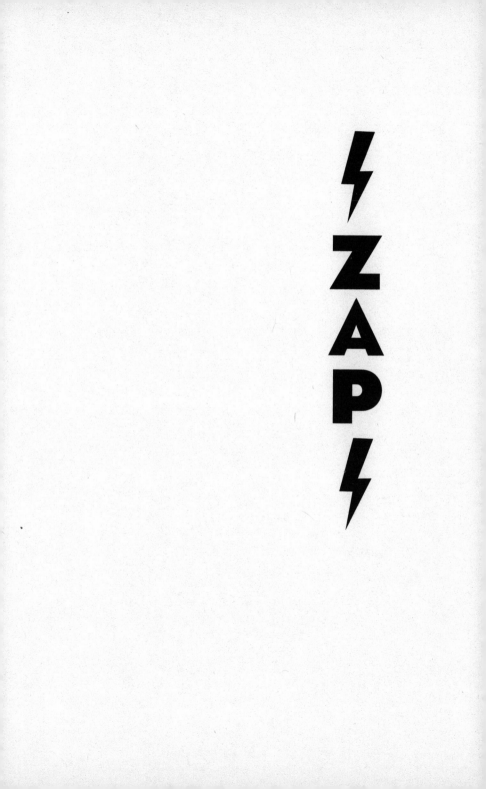

n a motel room somewhere in South Jersey, a skinny white guy known online as "plague-PJ" lay in a bed, his laptop propped against his knees. On the nightstand beside him were a liter bottle of Mountain Dew and an open bag of nacho-cheese-flavored Doritos. The skinny guy licked orange dust off his fingertips, added a period to the e-mail he was writing, and then, without hesitation, hit send.

It was two fifteen in the afternoon. At New Jersey Light's offices in Hampton, New Jersey, a payroll technician sat at his desk. He was bored, struggling to stay awake, when an e-mail landed in his in-box. The sender appeared to be a friend he hadn't heard from in a long time, someone he knew from high school.

Time for the reunion? he wondered, and opened the e-mail: *Hey, how u doing? You heard I got puppy? Here are some pix.*

The payroll technician remembered, or thought he did, that his friend always did love dogs. Without thinking further, he clicked on the link. It would be a nice break from spreadsheets.

The puppy was a black Lab—adorable.

Meanwhile, back in his motel room, the skinny guy, who had been monitoring New Jersey Light's network, took a swig of Mountain Dew and smiled. The RAT had been dropped. *Lights out, Hampton*, he thought. *Zap.*

CHAPTER ONE

Luis hit the button again, hit it hard. Still, the bulb stayed unlit. This close to throwing the whole thing across the room, he stopped himself. If the noise woke his mom, she'd be mad. She was back on nights.

What Luis did instead was grab his phone and call the only other person he knew who had entered the science fair—Maura Brown.

"Did you follow the directions?" she asked.

"Yeah, I did. There's gremlins in the wires or something."

Luis Cardenal was eleven and in sixth grade. He was average height. His shoulders were beginning to broaden, but he still looked more skinny than strong. Luis had a mane of black hair and eyes that were almost as dark. His mom said he'd be a good-looking kid—guapísimo—if only he'd get a haircut and maybe smile once in a while.

When his mom said that, Luis pulled his lips back

from those teeth and made what Maura called his fierce face. This was a joke between them but not entirely a joke. Luis wasn't really angry the way he looked. More like he was determined, and the smile his mom wished for did not fit with determined.

Maura was Luis's best friend. *Ex*–best friend. Ex-best but still friend. Her hair was red-blond and thick. She had pale skin with freckles, and her eyes were blue. Her nose was so small that Luis had asked her once how she even breathed out of it.

She had socked him in reply, and he'd never asked again.

Now she said, "There are no gremlins."

"Maybe not in *your* science fair project," Luis said.

"It's a science fair project?" Maura said. "How lame is that—a lightbulb?"

"A lightbulb that won't light," Luis clarified. "So what's yours that's so great?"

"It's a replica of the first kidney dialysis machine," Maura said. "This Dutch doctor invented it right before the Nazi invasion. I mean, mine's going to be smaller and you can't hook it to a live body, or anything, but it turns out to be not that hard to build. You get plastic wrap and orange juice cans—"

Luis stopped listening. The Nazi part had sounded interesting, but he didn't know what a di-whatzit machine was, and he sure as heck wasn't going to ask. Maura had a lot to say about her project, so while not listening he fiddled with the faulty circuit that lay in front of him on the floor of his blue bedroom—dark blue for Blue Lu.

It had taken a lot of talking, but finally last spring Luis had convinced his parents to let him claim the big bedroom that used to belong to his older brother, Reynaldo. Then he had hung up some posters scrounged from here and there—LeBron James, Kyrie Irving, Steph Curry. On his desk was a chessboard set up for a game. Reynaldo had promised Luis he would teach him to play; Luis was still waiting. The carpet on which he sat now was brown and threadbare, flattened by the soles of countless shoes.

There was a one-hundred-dollar prize if you won the science fair. It was definitely worth a try. To get what he needed for the project, Luis had braved the basement. Most of it was junk down there, but if you were determined, you could find almost anything—in this case electrical wire from the cord of a busted lamp, a nine-volt battery, a switch, and a bulb from an old flashlight. Luis had followed directions looked up online to create a circuit—battery connected to wire connected to switch connected to bulb, then back to wire and battery.

Maybe the battery was dead? But it looked brand-new.

Now Maura was talking about kidneys. Luis had heard somewhere that you could test a battery with your tongue. It sounded weird, but—*"Ow!"*

"Luis! Are you okay?" Maura's voice came from the floor.

"Thorry," Luis said, his tongue not working right, then, "Thorry," again when he had picked the phone up. "Don't evuh wick a battewy, Mauwa. It huwts—and it tastes tew-wibuh."

"Why would I do anything that dumb?" Maura asked.

"No reason." The terrible taste was still there, but his tongue was recovering.

"Do you want me to come over and take a look at your project? Is that why you called?" Maura asked.

"You sound like a mom on TV, Maura: 'Don't make me come down there!'" said Luis.

There was a pause. Was she insulted?

Anyway, the fact was he *did* want Maura to come over. Who else was going to help him? Reynaldo would have, but he'd be at work at the garage. He worked all the time.

Luis's parents were working, too, and anyway what did they know about science fair projects? They had gone to school in a Nicaraguan village. According to them, the school had dirt floors and one beat-up science book the whole class had to share.

"Forget it," he told Maura. "I'll figure it out, or I won't. You're right. It's a stupid project anyway."

"I've got my bike," Maura said. "I'll be there soon."

CHAPTER TWO

Maura fixed the circuit.

"There was gunk in the switch, see?" Maura showed Luis. "So it wasn't making contact, and the circuit wasn't complete. You get it how it works, right?"

"Yeah, sure," Luis said. "The negatively charged particles—electrons, right?—they move from one battery poll through the wire toward the positively charged particles in the other poll. On the way, they heat the filament in the bulb to make light."

"If you break the circuit, the electrons stop, and the light goes off," Maura said.

Luis nodded, and then he had a fine idea. "You know something, Maura? I am really impressed with how clearly you understand this *and* how clearly you can explain it."

"You want something, don't you?" Maura said.

"What? No! Of course not," Luis said, "only, uh . . .

you could help me write my summary. With your outstanding skills, it'll turn out great. Maybe I'll even win."

Luis Cardenal could not remember a time he hadn't known Maura Brown. He was born two weeks before her at the same hospital. They had gone to the same day care, preschool, and now elementary school. In a year they would move to St. Ignatius together—provided his grades were good enough. You had to be smart to go to St. Ignatius.

Maura used to live in Hampton, too, but the spring before, her family—her mom, her big sister, Beth, and her grandpa—had moved to a subdivision just outside the city limits.

"Maura's grandpa must be getting a nice pension from the power company," Luis's mom guessed when Luis told her. "That's how they could afford it."

"Can I go visit?" Luis had asked.

"¿Por qué no?—why not, if she invites you," his mom had said.

When Maura did invite him, he reported back, "The house is gigantic, new paint and fluffy carpets. They have a yard with grass and even a huge old tree. There are three bathrooms. I wish we could move there."

"Maybe you will someday," his mom had said, "when

you grow up and go to college and get a good job—a clean job at a desk."

Now Maura told Luis she didn't have time to help him write his summary.

"Mom's at work," she explained, "and my grandpa's got a headache. I told him I'd come home and make him something to eat."

Luis couldn't think of a way to argue with that.

"Hasta luego, in that case," he said. "But maybe later in the week? The summary's not due yet, right?"

"Friday," Maura said. "And maybe you could help me out too."

"Sure!" Luis hoped his enthusiasm didn't sound too fake. "I always wanted to know more about kidneys."

CHAPTER THREE

When Luis Cardenal was seven years old, he had set a house on fire.

It was his first time on his own exploring one of the abandoned houses in his neighborhood. The houses were off-limits, of course, but that didn't stop Luis or his brother or their friends either. That day he was going to try roasting marshmallows the way the kids did in a story his teacher had read at school.

He had been careful—for real. He had mounded twigs and newspaper on a double sheet of foil in what used to be a living room. He had lit the wannabe campfire with a match and grinned when it burst into flame.

But he was just a little kid. How was he supposed to know the fire would burn through the foil and ignite what was left of the rug?

Luis had torn off his T-shirt to smother the flames, but the shirt caught fire too. When that happened, he did the first smart thing he'd done all day, he ran—but not before grabbing the marshmallows.

A neighbor had seen the smoke and called 911. Fire trucks had come and put down the flames before they got out of control. Months later wreckers came and demolished what was left of the house.

Luis told only one person what had happened, his brother, Reynaldo, and Reynaldo had kept the secret—on two conditions.

First, he wanted the rest of the marshmallows. Luis hadn't minded handing them over that much. They were beginning to get stale.

Second, Reynaldo made Luis promise he would never play with matches again. "I will kill you if you do," Reynaldo said, "¿Entiendes? Now promise!"

"I promise," Luis had said. It was a promise he had kept.

On Monday morning Luis awoke with his alarm, batted the clock to turn it off, counted three-two-one, bent knees to chest, and kicked—vaulting himself out of bed.

The way Luis saw it, fate hadn't given him the advantages it gave other kids—the ones in the shows he watched, the ones his teachers made him read about, the ones who lived in houses like Maura's—so he would take those advantages for himself. Every day he got up planning to beat the day before it could beat him.

At Dudley School the first bell was at 8:10. The walk from home was four blocks, and Luis had the timing down to a science: It took ten minutes to get there if he didn't stop for an extra breakfast of gummi worms at Señora Álvaro's bodega, thirteen minutes if he did.

At 7:35 Luis headed for the kitchen. He was clean and dressed and more or less combed. Luis's dad would already have been through by this time. Luis's dad left the house before six because construction work started early. Luis's mom, having worked overnight, would still be in bed.

Luis opened the cupboard by the sink and made a happy discovery, a new box of Pop-Tarts—and not just Kellogg's either, the expensive organic kind. Luis's brother, Reynaldo, must have dropped them off. Only his brother would be so extravagant. Luis's mom believed off-brand corn flakes were fine. "They're the same thing," she said. "If you want to be fancy, add sugar."

"Thank you, Jesus, for Reynaldo," Luis mumbled. Then he put two Pop-Tarts in the toaster and a mug of water in the microwave for instant coffee. It was 7:42—Luis would always remember that. He had just pressed the start button when the clock blinked twice and went black. At the same time the toaster popped and the fridge's hum went silent.

When he looked back later, Luis realized he should've known right away that the power was out. Instead he felt baffled. The world was acting screwy. *What the heck?*

Then his brain kicked in. Had he tripped the circuit breaker when he turned on the microwave? After yesterday, he actually understood this. The electricity in his house was organized into circuits like the one he had built. There was one for the bathroom, one for the bedrooms, one for the kitchen, and so on. If there was more electricity flowing than the circuit could carry, like in the bathroom when the hair dryer and space heater were on at the same time, a switch flipped to break the circuit and stop the flow. Otherwise, overloaded wires might get so hot they melted.

Luis didn't go to the basement to check the panel. His mom could do it when she got up. Instead, he drank grainy, lukewarm coffee and ate a half-raw Pop-Tart. Then he tugged on his camo-print backpack and headed out the front door, down two steps to the sidewalk, and turned left—away from the river—toward Dudley School.

CHAPTER FOUR

I t was late October. The morning was cool, the sky brightening to brilliant daytime blue. Luis walked without paying much attention to the neighborhood around him. What was there to see? Brick or vinyl-sided row houses like his own—many of them vacant and boarded up, cracked sidewalks, dog waste nobody bothered to pick up, weeds sprouting in the gutters.

Besides the usual fast-food wrappers and beer cans, the litter that morning included red-white-and-blue campaign flyers: JULIA GIRARDO FOR MAYOR, SHE'S GOT ALL THE ANSWERS!

From social studies, Luis knew the election was coming up in November. He wondered if Julia Girardo really expected anyone around here to read the flyers. A lot of the adults were sin papeles—undocumented immigrants—and they weren't allowed to vote. Most of the rest were probably like Reynaldo and their parents. They didn't see what politics had to do with them.

Señora Álvaro's bodega was the halfway point on Luis's walk. When it came into view, he realized something was truly wrong. Usually the open sign in the window was a colorful beacon, but not today. Today it was dark—and come to think of it, why were so many drivers honking their horns?

So the power outage hadn't been only in Luis's own kitchen, or only in his own house either. It seemed to be all over the neighborhood, maybe all over town.

Luis checked the time on his phone. If he hurried, he could check in with Señora Álvaro—get the news and maybe some gummi worms too. Señora Álvaro always knew what was going on.

"Buenos días, buenas noches—good morning, good night," she greeted him. She had a candle lit beside the dead cash register. The only other light was daylight streaming through cloudy windows. "How long do you think this is going to last, anyway?"

"That's what I came in to ask you," Luis said.

"I got some news off the phone," said the señora. "They say it's only part of the city now, but it's getting bigger—*cascading*, they said. Is there a hurricane nobody told me about?"

Luis shrugged. "It's sort of like a mystery, I guess."

"Yeah, okay, so I got a favor to ask," said Señora Álvaro. "I need a big strong kid to take something to the genius. I don't have a big strong kid, so you will have to do."

Luis was used to the señora's sense of humor. "I got school," he said. "I can't be late. I'm never late."

"One time you can be. It's an emergency," Señora Álvaro said.

Luis made a quick decision. Arguing would only waste time and make him later. "What is it I'm delivering?"

"Get a quart of chocolate milk from the case there." Señora Álvaro handed him a bag. "He needs milk to keep him alive."

Luis couldn't believe it. "Are you kidding me? I'm gonna be late to school for the first time in my life because—"

Señora Álvaro shut him down with a look. She was old, an abuela many times over, but her hair was jet black and pulled tight in a bun. Luis was an average-height kid, and she was half a head shorter. That made her tiny, Luis guessed, only no one thought of her that way. Everyone counted on her and her bodega.

"Go find him," Señora Álvaro said. "What are you good for if you can't? Maybe I'll give you some gummi worms when you get back. How would you like that?"

"I'm not coming back. I'm going to school. Where is the genius anyway?"

"¿Quién sabe?—who knows?" she said. "Aren't you supposed to be smart? Go out and find him."

Luis unzipped his backpack, put the quart of milk inside, and ran. *Why did I stop, anyway?* he asked himself.

Unlike most legends, the genius—aka Computer Genius—actually existed. The story went that he was a bad little kid who ran away from home and turned up eventually in one of the abandoned houses.

He had gotten hold of a laptop—how? He had taught himself to program—how? It was true that even in poor neighborhoods, Wi-Fi signals bounced everywhere. He had learned the secret of intercepting them and spent his days and nights online. Sometimes he did jobs for people like Señora Álvaro. Maybe she paid him in chocolate milk.

You could call the genius homeless or many-homed. Either way, he migrated. There were half a dozen likely prospects near the señora's bodega, and Luis checked them all in a hurry. He was looking for telltale signs of the genius in residence, fast-food cups outside, candy wrappers, a window cleaned off so you could see out of it. If the genius was feeling good, he might tack some old tablecloth up to serve as a curtain.

Luis ran from likely house to likely house, rejecting each one and working up a sweat. All the while he felt time passing. Eight ten was the first bell and eight fifteen the second. If he got to school after eight twenty-five, he'd have to get a pass from the office, and that meant dealing with the school secretary. He did not want to do that. The last time he'd needed a late pass was when he was in fourth grade. Back then his dad drove him to school, and his dad had overslept. The secretary must have been in a chatty mood that morning because she asked him what Nicaraguans eat for breakfast.

"I'm not Nicaraguan," Luis had told her.

"Oh—my bad," the secretary had said. "I always thought that's where your family came from."

"I come from right here in New Jersey," Luis said. "I'm American."

The school secretary had frowned, apparently not liking this answer. "You should watch your attitude," she'd said.

When Luis imagined getting a tattoo someday, that's what it would say: You should watch your attitude. It was 8:20 when Luis suspended his search for Computer Genius. He felt bad, but he would try again after school. A few more hours without chocolate milk wouldn't hurt, would it?

CHAPTER FIVE

At the big intersection across from Dudley School, the traffic lights were out. Some white guy wearing a gray coat and an Eagles cap—not a cop—was directing traffic. To Luis's surprise, most of the drivers obeyed.

Late as he was, Luis thought this over. *Does the guy know what he's doing? What if he waved go when he should've waved stop? Would the drivers crash into each other, or think for themselves?*

Dudley School was a tall, stark, unfriendly building with bars on the windows and an asphalt playground. The school had been built to educate twice as many kids as now attended. So many empty classrooms, closets, and corridors almost made the place feel haunted. In kindergarten, Luis had had nightmares about ghosts and sharp-toothed teachers. Now the school looked the same as usual but with one difference—kids and teachers were all outside on the playground.

Luis breathed a sigh of relief. The power outage must have silenced the bells and undone the schedule too. He was almost half an hour late, and it didn't matter.

"Hey, hue." Luis's cousin Carlos slapped him on the back as soon as he came through the gate. "Where you been anyway? It's crazy about the power, am I right?"

"Crazy, hue," Luis agreed. In Hampton, the Latino kids called each other "hue," pronounced "way," like kids elsewhere called each other "dude" or "bro."

"And how are they gonna teach us without electricity?" Carlos went on. "My eyes are delicate; they can't read in the dark."

In Luis's experience, the word "cousin" applied to anybody whose relatives came from more or less the same place as yours, but Carlos was a real cousin—Luis's dad's sister's kid. He was also Luis's best friend now that Maura had been demoted. In some ways, Carlos was Luis's opposite—softer, rounder, and less coordinated. His default setting was cheerful. Once Maura had called him a teddy bear to his face and he hadn't even minded.

Speaking of Maura—here she was beside them on the blacktop, looking at her phone. "Late bell should've rung by now," she announced. "They'll have to send us home if the power doesn't come back. It's too dangerous to keep us in a dark school. Not to mention the toilets won't flush."

"Ewww—TMI," said Carlos.

"Why won't they flush?" Luis asked.

"You have to pump the water to the higher floors, and that takes electricity," Maura said. "The water pressure already in the system will keep it working for a while, not for long."

"How do you even know this stuff?" Luis asked.

Maura tapped the side of her head. "Brains up to here."

Carlos laughed. Luis ignored the comment, but then he thought of something. "Have you called your mom?" he asked Maura. "Is she working?"

"I tried but no answer. She must be super busy," Maura said.

"During that big storm that time, didn't she work, like, two days straight?" Luis asked.

"Three," said Maura. "They set up cots so she and the other dispatchers could take naps."

"What's her job again?" Carlos asked.

"She's a dispatcher for NJL—New Jersey Light," Maura explained. "She watches the electricity. If something goes wrong, she makes adjustments to fix it."

"So it looks like today she messed up," Carlos said.

Now Luis laughed—and Maura gave Carlos a dangerous look.

"Kidding! I'm kidding!" Carlos said. "Uh . . . so how does that job work anyway?"

"Never mind," Maura said.

"No, seriously." Carlos could be very sincere when he wanted to be. "I wanna know."

Maura shrugged. "There's something called SCADA—S-C-A-D-A. I can't remember what it stands for. The idea is there are sensors on the poles and in the transformers. You know, those big can things up on the poles?"

Carlos nodded, but anyone could tell he had no idea what she was talking about.

"The sensors see if something's wrong, and then they talk to the computers," Maura said. "Simple."

"Simple, Carlos, right?" Luis elbowed his cousin.

"Exactamente," Carlos said.

Up till this point, the Dudley playground hubbub had been pretty much the same as it was on any other day. But now kids were quieting down. When Luis looked, he realized it was because Principal Simon—a tall black woman who wore blazers in every kind of weather—had appeared on the steps that led to the school's entrance. Her hands were raised for silence, and for once kids paid attention.

Luis thought about the drivers at the intersection again. Maybe there was something about an emergency—even a dinky emergency like the power being out—that made people do what they were told.

"I am sorry to inform you," Principal Simon said, "that the district has asked us, due to the uncertainty surrounding the timing of the restoration of electricity, to dismiss school early today. Now, Dudley students, if you will all please line up by class for checkout with your teachers . . ."

Joyful shouts and *woo-woo-woo*s resounded from the high flat face of the building. Was Luis imagining it, or were the teachers smiling most broadly of all? He for sure saw the school nurse, Miss Rivera, high-five the kindergarten aide, Mrs. Lynley.

Principal Simon went on to talk about contacting parents, after-school child care, bus schedules, e-mailing parents, and so on. None of this mattered to him, to Carlos, or to Maura. None of their parents would be coming to get them. It had been years since they'd gone to after-school child care. So, like almost all the other kids sixth grade and older, they ignored the rest of what Mrs. Simon was saying and filed out the open gate. The teachers were too busy herding younger kids to stop them.

So far, Luis thought, this power outage deal was great.

arlos announced he was going home to play video games.

"For real, Carlos?" Maura said. "Your screen is plugged into the wall, right?"

Carlos looked puzzled. "Yeah, so . . . *oh,*" he said. "Right. But I bet by the time I get home the electricity will be back. It's not like there's a snowstorm. Your mom and her SCUD computer will fix it right away."

"SCADA," said Maura. "And you're right. Probably a squirrel."

"What do you mean, a squirrel?" Luis said.

"Squirrels cause a lot of outages. They gnaw on the lines and cause short circuits."

"I've always heard that—short circuit—but I never knew what it meant," Carlos said.

"I know! I know!" Luis raised his hand the way the obnoxious kids did, the ones who wanted to act smart so teachers would like them. He didn't like those kids. "It means the electricity goes the wrong way, follows a path it's not supposed to."

"Like into the body of a cute, furry *squirrel*?" Carlos said.

Maura drew her finger across her throat. "And out the other end. Rest in peace, little buddy. You are officially zapped."

Carlos was wide-eyed. "That's terrible!"

"The human body is a pathway for electricity too," Maura said. "It conducts electricity, in other words. That's why people get hurt when they touch a live power line. The electricity goes right through you to the ground—or whatever else you're touching."

"Also, I have it on good authority that you get hurt if you lick a battery," Luis added. "Not that I know anyone stupid enough to do that."

"Don't tell me any more." Carlos put his hands over his ears. "You are messing with my understanding of the universe, and there's only so much of that I can stand. Anyway, I am going home. When the power comes back, I want to be in position on the couch with snacks ready."

After Carlos took off, Luis felt awkward standing with

Maura on the sidewalk by the school. It was random that the two of them had ended up here together. Till yesterday, they hadn't been spending much time together. "Uh, so what are you doing now?" Luis asked after a minute.

"Going home, I guess," Maura said. "Wanna come? We've got a battery radio. We can find out what's going on."

"I've got my phone. I don't need a radio," Luis said.

"You've got your phone till it dies," Maura said.

"You really think the blackout will last that long?" Luis asked.

"It's good to be prepared," Maura said. "The radio has a crank on it too—a generator, I mean. Turn the crank and it's supposed to work forever."

"Cool," said Luis. He had never seen a radio like that. Also Maura's house was nice, and there would be good snacks. Still, he did not want anyone he knew to see him leave with a girl. So he glanced around to make sure nobody was looking.

Maura frowned. "You don't *have* to come home with me, you know. There's plenty of other people I'd rather hang with—pretty much everybody, now that I think—"

"Yeah, no. Sorry," Luis said. It was annoying that she

saw through him. "So let's go and let's hurry, okay? Maybe there's ice cream in your freezer. Melting ice cream."

Maura smiled. "If Beth didn't eat it first. She loves ice cream."

"I thought Beth was away at college," Luis said.

"She's home this semester. She's got an internship with the police department," Maura said.

"That's cool, I guess," Luis said, but in truth he was no fan of the police. It was different for Maura, but for him and most of the other people in his neighborhood, the police were the ones who took parents or friends away. Some of them were deported and never came back. Maura got her bike, and the two of them started walking back to Luis's house so they could pick up his. There was a hand-scrawled sign on the door at Señora Álvaro's bodega: STILL OPEN. CASH ONLY. FREEZER ITEMS HALF OFF.

Shoot, Luis thought, remembering Computer Genius and the chocolate milk in his backpack. Now he had time to seek him out. But he couldn't do that with Maura. She wasn't the kind of kid who went exploring abandoned houses. He would have to come back later.

At his house, he told Maura he'd be right back and went to grab his bike. Inside, it was quiet, which meant his mom was still in bed. The meatpacking plant where she worked was just north of town. Luis wondered if it would have to shut down for the day. You couldn't pack meat in the dark, and the cutting machines and conveyor belt ran on electricity.

So far the blackout was no big deal—a day off from school. But what if it turned out to be bigger than he realized? A lot of things ran on electricity. What happened if it didn't come back on? How had people lived before electricity anyway?

Luis's bike hung on a hook on the wall of his bedroom. Carrying it through the living room, he heard something through the window, a crackle-distorted voice over a loudspeaker.

Back outside, he followed Maura's gaze and saw a red pickup truck with a speaker on the hood moving very slowly down the street. The windshield was tinted, but Luis could make out the driver, a bald guy who seemed to have been stuffed into his black shirt. In the truck bed, a blond woman wearing a red jacket and blue slacks was yelling into a microphone and waving as if there were a crowd.

Only there wasn't a crowd. There was only Luis and Maura.

"Who the heck's *that*?" Luis asked, but then he saw campaign posters plastered all over the truck: JULIA GIRARDO FOR MAYOR: SHE'S GOT ALL THE ANSWERS!

". . . a power outage of unprecedented scale," she was saying, ". . . the most important message is that we must not panic, amigos. No matter how much you miss your light, your heat, your precious televisions—this is the time for action! Fight back against the shocking deterioration of our city, deterioration that the current mayor has allowed to take place! Now, does anyone have a question? Because Julia Girardo has answers! Young man!" She waved at Luis. "Do you have a question?"

"Me?" Luis looked around like he was sure she meant someone else. "Uh, no. I don't."

"You keep thinking, then, young man!" Julia Girardo smiled and waved some more. After that, mercifully for Maura and Luis's eardrums, the truck continued down the street.

When it was gone, Luis shook his head. "Never saw anything like that."

"Me neither," Maura said, "but I guess the power outage is the mayor's fault."

"Is that what she said?" Luis asked.

Maura shrugged. "Something like that."

"The longer it lasts, the more ice cream and the less school," Luis said. "Are you ready to go?"

"Vamonos," said Maura.

"Don't even try," said Luis. "Your Spanish is terrible."

"Gracias muchísimas," said Maura.

Luis made a face and shook his head.

CHAPTER SEVEN

The bike ride to Maura's house took only twenty minutes, but the change of scenery was dramatic. First the narrow streets of Luis's neighborhood fed into boulevards lined with strip malls and Wawa stores, then to a highway with big-box stores and parking lots big as dairy farms on either side. Past the big mall were a few actual farms, where you could pick your own blueberries in the summer and pears in the fall.

Finally, you made a turn and arrived all at once in a land of four-bedroom houses, lawns and trees, flowers and driveways.

By now the power had been out for almost four hours. Luis had expected it might be on once they left the city, but it wasn't. Wherever they went, police officers were directing traffic at major intersections, their cars pulled to the shoulder of the road, light bars flashing. The smaller bodegas had CLOSED signs in the windows; none of the gas stations had customers, and most looked deserted.

For the time being, there was less traffic than usual, but Luis wondered how long that would last. Would people pack up and leave if the power stayed out? Where would they go?

How far did the blackout extend anyway?

Luis had been to visit los tíos in New York City. He knew this was the road you took to get to the New Jersey Turnpike. It was quiet now, but he could imagine it bumper-to-bumper with cars on their way to someplace with electricity, someplace normal.

The blackout made Luis notice something he'd never thought about: the countless power lines along the roadways, suspended by countless poles and towers. Inside them, electrons had fallen down on the job. They were supposed to be buzzing from atom to atom, negative charges seeking their positive partners. Only now the electrons were still. "Hey, Maura!" he hollered.

Riding a few yards ahead, she looked over her shoulder, then dropped back. There was so little traffic that they could ride side by side. "What? I'm right here. You don't have to shout," she said.

"Do you know a lot about electricity?" Luis asked. "I

mean, like, do you know what those barrel things are on the power poles?"

Maura glanced up. "Sure," she said, "but I can't believe you care. I mean, now that your circuit is built."

"I don't," Luis assured her. "I'm only curious. I mean, I wouldn't mind getting my 'precious television' back, like the mayor lady said. Or maybe tonight I might want to read a book and it'll be dark and I can't. So if that happens, I might want to know why."

"Right—*you're* gonna want to read a book," said Maura.

"Call it a hypothetical—if you know that word," Luis said.

Maura was right that reading was not Luis's favorite pastime. He liked beating someone in a race or eating his mom's ceviche, a Nicaraguan specialty. He liked video games sometimes, and exploring abandoned houses. But Tía Laura—she had been a teacher in Nicaragua—had given him a book of Greek myths, and when one night he'd been bored enough to open it, he'd realized the stories were awesome, with more gore than a Texas chain saw ever inflicted.

Also, the gods were like kick-butt superheroes.

Later, when Tía Laura had given him another Greek book, *The Odyssey*, about a general sailing home after a war, he'd read that too. The story had words he didn't understand, but he liked the general for keeping cool and thinking straight even when he was threatened by monsters, sorcerers, and gods.

It seemed to Luis that keeping cool was key if you wanted to be a hero.

"God, you're annoying, Luis," Maura said. "And yes, I know that word. And I know what the 'barrel' things are too. They're called step-down transformers."

"Like what you were talking about at school—with sensors in them," Luis said.

"I can't believe you were listening," Maura said.

"Ears were a wonderful invention," said Luis. "So what do the transformers transform?"

"Electric current," Maura said. "There are coils of wire inside that *transform* it from the high voltage that runs through the power line to lower voltage for your house. Otherwise the electricity would fry your precious TV and melt your wires too."

Luis thought this was pretty interesting. In fact, he wouldn't mind knowing more. Wasn't there a nuclear power plant nearby? How did you get electricity from nuclear power—from atoms? It sounded dangerous but also cool. Was that electricity radioactive? If it was, shouldn't the power lines be glowing?

He decided not to ask Maura any more questions, though. He wouldn't want her to turn into one of those know-it-all kids, the ones that waved their hands to be called on. He had to protect her from herself.

By now they were almost to Maura's turnoff, and she stood up on her pedals to pull ahead. Lean right, make the turn, one more street and three houses down, she rode into the driveway and jumped off her bike. Luis was right behind her.

Maura's house was two stories with puffball yellow flowers lining the front walk, a patch of mostly green grass, and a big tree shading the front yard. Luis looked up into the branches and wondered if owning a tree meant you owned the squirrels and the birds' nests too.

"It's an elm," Maura said.

"I know it's an elm," Luis said, even though he didn't. "What do you think? I don't know trees?"

"And those flowers are mums, and these plants with the long, striped leaves are hostas, and this kind of grass is called fescue," Maura said. "That's all stuff I've learned since we moved out here."

"Well, aren't you fancy?" Luis said.

"Fancier every day," Maura said. "Don't you want to move out of Hampton someday?"

Of course he did, and he wanted to go to college too—maybe West Point, which was where the army sent you. He wasn't sure where West Point was, but it sure as heck wasn't Hampton.

Luis wasn't ready to share his plans. Maura would probably laugh. "Too fancy for me," he said.

Meanwhile, Maura had pulled her keys from a zipper pocket in her backpack, opened the door, and flipped a light switch in the dark hallway.

Then she laughed at herself because, of course, the hallway stayed dark.

"Beth, are you home?" Maura called, but there was no answer.

Luis pulled out his phone, swiped to turn on the flashlight and shined the beam around. The only other time Luis had been here, there was plastic on the chairs and boxes were stacked everywhere. But now Maura, her mom, and sister were settled in, with pictures on the wall and her mom's collection of ceramic poodles on display in a cabinet.

"You're wasting the battery, you know," Maura said.

"Aw, it doesn't matter," Luis said. "The power'll be back soon."

Maura shrugged. "I hope. For now we've got a closet full of batteries and lanterns and that kind of stuff. We've even got bottled water."

Luis frowned. "Why would we need that?"

"Not sure exactly," Maura admitted. "Something to do with how it takes electricity to run the water plant, so it gets polluted when the electricity goes out. My grandpa explained, but I didn't really listen."

"High-five, Maura Brown!" said Luis. "I thought you always listened to grown-ups. I didn't know you were mortal like the rest of us."

"Very funny, Luis Cardenal," Maura said.

"What else you got in that closet?" Luis asked.

"Come and look."

The closet was halfway down the hall that led to the bedrooms. When Maura opened the door, Luis saw a shelf of plastic containers with labels: CANDLES, BATTERIES, MATCHES, FLASHLIGHTS, WATER. On another shelf was a camp stove and four lanterns—two kerosene and two battery-powered. There were also four cardboard cartons labeled MRE, VARIETY PACK, EXP 9/2050.

"Wow—what *is* all this stuff?" Luis grabbed a big black radio with a hand crank on the side and a shiny, flat panel on the top.

"I told you already," Maura said. "It's a radio made so you can charge it with the sun—that's a solar panel on the top—or with the hand crank."

"That is so cool," Luis said. "Let's try it."

"We can go outside where it's light," Maura said.

On the way to the patio, Luis realized he didn't under-stand how the crank made electricity or how the sun did either—more things he had never thought about till now with power gone. Not having something focused your mind, he thought, like how you think of nothing but food when you're hungry.

Outside, the only furniture was a plastic picnic table with benches. They sat down, and Maura fiddled with the radio. It came on with a crackle of static followed by the clear sound of a baby crying and then a woman's crabby voice: "Oh! Do please take him back if he's going to bawl. *Please!*" Luis and Maura both recognized the ad before the announcer's voice came on: "We'll all be crying if Julia Girardo is elected. Return Mayor Adam Manuel to office this November."

Luis made a face. "*Ow*—that ad is hard on the eardrums. Who wants to hear a baby cry anyway?"

"That's the whole point," said Maura. "That Julia lady made the baby cry; therefore she must be bad."

"Does that even make any sense?" Luis asked.

"Yeah, no—who knows? It's politics," said Maura. "People say whatever they want, at least according to my mom."

"My parents say politicians work for rich folks. Rich like you, I guess."

"We're not rich," said Maura.

"Good joke, Maura. Look around compared to where you used to live—to where I still live," Luis said.

"Lots of people are richer than us—lots and *lots* of people," Maura said.

Luis could tell Maura felt uncomfortable. "It's not like this is a mansion exactly," he admitted.

"No, it's not," Maura said. "And I don't think politicians are all bad either."

Luis shrugged. He didn't know enough to win the

argument. "Anyway, that lady—the one who made the baby cry—she's the one we saw on the truck, right? She wants to be mayor."

"Yeah, I think," said Maura. "And somebody handed her their baby for a picture, and the baby screamed and the other guy—the guy who's mayor now, the guy who's running against her—made an ad out of it."

"It is kind of funny," Luis admitted. "Hang on, here's news about the blackout. Listen."

". . . a spokesman for NJL, New Jersey Light, says crews are working around the clock, but as yet no cause has been identified for the outage and no estimate is available for power restoration. Asked if terrorism has been ruled out, the spokesman said only 'No comment.'

"Repeating the day's top story: An estimated five hundred and fifty thousand South Jersey businesses and households over an area of more than twenty-five hundred square miles are without electricity at the present time as a result of a blackout that stopped clocks shortly before eight this morning.

"So far no deaths or serious injuries have been blamed on the outage, but there are dozens of reports of people stuck in elevators while overstretched crews try to reach them. Emergency generators are powering hospitals, broadcasters, police and fire departments, and other critical facilities at present.

"Should the power outage persist beyond the twenty-four-hour mark, fuel shortages could develop, causing further complications and possibly health risks.

"The city and county's office of emergency management advises listeners to stay home if possible, stay calm, and stay tuned in right here at 104.5, WJZY."

A commercial for diabetes medicine came on, and Luis turned the volume down. "It sounds like we can do our part by eating ice cream," he said.

"It won't be melted yet," said Maura.

"Who wants to eat ice cream soup?" Luis said.

"Truth," said Maura. "Let's see what's in the freezer."

The answer was strawberry ice cream. Without light, they had to root around a minute before they found it though. They got spoons from a drawer and went back outside to share it from the carton. It hadn't gone soupy yet. In fact, it was delicious.

"I thought your grandpa was living with you too," Luis said after scraping up the last drips.

"He is," Maura said.

"So where is he?" Luis asked.

Maura shrugged. "I don't know. He has his own apartment over the garage. He's probably . . . Oh."

Luis read her mind. "You were going to say watching TV."

"Yeah, I was, but I guess not, right? That was his car in the driveway, though."

"Does he take walks or anything?" Luis asked.

"Ha!" said Maura. "My grandpa believes the recliner chair is man's greatest invention—right up there with football and color TV."

"My dad would tell you the same, but make it soccer and add cerveza—beer," Luis said.

"Maybe we should go say hi." Maura stood up again. "We can make sure he's okay."

"Why wouldn't he be?" Luis stood up too.

Maura shrugged. "He didn't feel that good yesterday. We go in through the back of the garage. It'll be dark, so I'll turn on the lantern. You're right. I'm sure he's okay."

CHAPTER EIGHT

But Maura's grandpa was not okay.

The door to his apartment was at the top of the stairs from the garage. Maura knocked again and again but got no answer. Then she remembered that her mom kept a spare key on a hook in a laundry room cupboard, so—while Luis stood on the landing and called through the closed door in the dark—she ran down and got it.

The blinds on the window that looked over the driveway were open, and Mr. O'Hara's apartment was much lighter than the landing. When the door opened, Luis was blinded by glare. Maura's eyes adjusted faster and she gasped.

"*Grandpa!*" she said, and rushed forward.

Mr. O'Hara was, as expected, seated in the recliner in his small sitting room. His eyes were open and he was turned toward the TV, watching the empty screen. At first

Luis couldn't see what had upset Maura. Her grandpa looked okay to him. But then Luis saw that he was slumped to one side, and his face looked strange, lopsided, as if the left half had collapsed. His eyes were blank. A line of drool extended from the corner of his mouth down his chin.

Maura took her grandfather's wrist. She must've remembered that day in health when they all checked one another's pulses.

Was Mr. O'Hara dead?

Luis held his breath, waiting for a pronouncement, but before Maura spoke, her grandpa blinked and tried to move his head.

"He'p me," he murmured.

"We're here, Grandpa," Maura said. "We will. Luis, call—"

Luis already had his phone out.

The 911 dispatch center didn't answer till the fifth ring, and then it was a recording: "All lines are busy due to the electrical emergency. If your need is not urgent, please hang up and try again later. If yours is a true emergency, please stay on the line and someone will be with you as soon as possible."

Waiting was terrible. Luis hated not doing anything, not

knowing what to do. Exasperation made his heart pound. Once he had seen a kid get shot—a drug deal and something went wrong; the kid was just unlucky. Hit, he squawked and fell, a bloom of blood on his sleeve. An older kid had known to cover the wound with a T-shirt, press hard to stop the bleeding. In the end the injured arm was patched up, and the kid wore his cast like a medal for bravery.

That had been scary, a shock. But not as bad as this. Mr. O'Hara looked strange and sick and helpless. He wasn't going to die, was he? He wasn't much older than Luis's dad.

After a couple of minutes, Maura pulled out her own phone and dialed her mom. "It's Grandpa," she said, and explained. "You are? Really? But what about . . . ? Oh. Okay—good. See you soon." She hung up and looked at Luis. "She's coming home. They told her to, which is weird but lucky for us—for *him*." She bent down and spoke into her grandfather's ear. "Hang on. You're gonna be okay."

Maura's grandpa blinked and moved his chin. Was he trying to say he understood? Then he moved his lips and with great effort made a sound—a single soft syllable.

Luis couldn't make it out. "What did he say?"

"I'm not sure," Maura said. "But it kind of sounded like 'zap.'"

CHAPTER NINE

While Maura sat with her grandpa, Luis packed a bag for him to take to the hospital. The way he was now, it was hard to imagine he would ever use his toothbrush or his razor, either. But the doctors would fix him up, right?

Maura's mom got home a few minutes later and charged up the stairs into the apartment. She cried when she saw her father. Maura barely had time to react before the ambulance screamed into the driveway. Soon the apartment exploded in a blur of hustle-bustle—EMTs in a hurry asking questions, attaching Grandpa to oxygen, strapping him to a gurney, muscling the gurney down the narrow stairs, and wheeling it toward the open doors of the ambulance.

Then, just as abruptly, it was quiet again. "Come with us to the hospital?" Maura said.

"I'll ride my bike and meet you," Luis answered. He

didn't know what use he would be, but he couldn't exactly abandon her, right?

This was the strangest day ever. Right about now he ought to have been on his way to lunch. When he imagined the Dudley cafeteria, warm and well lit and full of noise, it was like some other planet.

Whitman Hospital was in central Hampton, so Luis steered his bike toward home when he got out to the highway. As he rode, he noticed that the traffic was heavier than it had been earlier, and grocery store parking lots were full, with lines of shoppers snaking out the doors. This was how things were when a big storm was in the forecast. The shoppers Luis saw were toting cases of bottled water and carts full of toilet paper.

Luis had been to the hospital only one other time, when his dad fell off a ladder on a construction site and hurt his back. Still, he had seen plenty of hospital shows on TV. He knew what hospitals were supposed to be like—bright and busy and noisy with mechanical beeps and gurgles. Now it was nothing like that. There were people everywhere, lots of them, but they were unnaturally quiet, and the light was gloomy.

Mrs. Brown stayed with her father in the emergency

room while Maura and Luis sat in a waiting area outside. Two TVs hung from brackets in the wall, both turned off to conserve the emergency power. Most of the chairs were occupied, but with dying phones and no TV, people didn't seem to know where to look. Several people had solved the problem by dozing off.

Luis shifted in his seat to take his phone from his pocket, then remembered he was saving the battery and left it alone.

"You have done that two hundred times in the last five minutes," Maura said. "Could you quit? It's like you've got a twitch."

"I think I'm showing admirable restraint," Luis said. "There's no music. No games. No video. No texts. I'm bored."

"I wouldn't mind knowing when the power's coming back," Maura said. "I wonder if there's a TV that's on anywhere."

"I thought I saw one when I came in through the main lobby." Luis was already on his feet.

"I'll text my mom to tell her what we're doing," Maura said. "I hope her phone is still charged. Mine is right about half dead."

The lobby was on the same floor as the ER, but at the opposite end of the building. When they got there, Luis and Maura discovered they weren't the only ones craving news. A crowd of about twenty people were standing around watching the lonely powered-up TV set. Their faces were grim and intent as they stared at the power company spokesperson on the screen. She was Latina, with smooth light hair and straight teeth. She spoke in a soft, clear voice. Luis thought she was lucky that she couldn't see the frustration on the faces of the people around him. If she could, she might not seem so calm.

"What we can tell you," the woman was saying, "is that at seven forty-two this morning, an outage of unknown provenance began affecting NJL customers in central Hampton. The outage took the form of a cascading event, by which I mean its effects rolled outward, with customers losing electricity in waves."

"When will the power be back?" a reporter yelled from off camera.

"What caused the blackout?" someone else asked.

"Is it true a foreign government might be involved?"

"What's 'provenance'?" That was Luis's question. He was asking Maura, but a tall black man wearing scrubs answered, "A big word to fool the people."

Luis thought, *Not helpful,* but what he said was, "Oh."

The man looked down at Luis, and his expression softened. "It means they don't know what started it," he explained.

"Somebody knows," said a white woman wearing a Bernie for President T-shirt and purple sweatpants. "And somebody's covering it up. I never liked that Julia Girardo before, but she's right. There's terrorists everywhere and who knows what all. We need somebody tougher than ol' Adam in office, someone to protect us."

"Hey, hush—I want to hear this," said someone else.

"See?" The white woman sniffed. "We are all of us a little bit on edge."

Meanwhile, back on TV, the power company spokesperson took a couple of breaths and continued. "At the present time there remain many unknown unknowns, but we are confident—"

More interruptions from reporters:

"Do you have any comment on mayoral candidate Julia Girardo's allegations of deteriorating infrastructure?"

"Is it true the local grid is particularly vulnerable to attack?"

The power company spokesperson closed her eyes and took a breath. "Okay, folks, I'm calling it a wrap. Thanks very much. We'll have another update in an hour, or in the event of, uh . . . changing events."

With that, she gathered up her notes, hugged them to her chest, and strode away from the podium. Reporters continued to holler, but the station cut to a commercial about digestion. A lot of the people in the hospital lobby turned away, but Luis and Maura stayed put. Maybe there would be more news after the commercial.

Luis had felt bad for the woman trying to answer questions. He hoped he never had a job like that. But the lady wearing the Bernie shirt seemed to think she was hiding something. Was it an accident that the electricity was off? Or was it something else?

Luis thought about what he'd heard. A grid, okay, that was like the pattern on graph paper, a bunch of connected squares. So maybe the *power* grid was a bunch of interconnected circuits, like his science fair project, or his house, only bigger. And instead of lightbulbs or toasters or microwave ovens on the circuits, there were whole households, whole businesses, whole factories.

The wires on the poles outside, they were part of the

grid, right? Part of the network of circuits. And the battery? That was the power plant.

Reasoning had taken Luis that far when the commercials ended and the local news came back. Sitting behind a desk was an Asian woman. She also had smooth hair and straight teeth.

"If you're tuning in, officials so far blame several accidents on the power outage still gripping the region at this hour," she said. "A fifty-four-year-old woman was seriously injured this morning when her 2005 Chevy Cavalier was struck by another vehicle at an intersection where traffic signals were out.

"Two more people, a man and a woman, both elderly, were found unconscious after relatives failed to contact them. Apparently, the backup power to their breathing apparatuses failed. They are currently being treated at Whitman Hospital. As you heard from NJL spokeswoman—"

"This is bad," Maura said.

Luis shook his head. "I always thought disasters were like storms and bombs and earthquakes. I never thought of this."

When commercials came on, Luis and Maura returned to the emergency room waiting area. Mrs. Brown was there, giving information to a clerk writing on a clipboard. The clerk kept apologizing for how long it was taking. The hospital had generators providing emergency power, she said, but there were problems with the Internet connection, and some of the computers were down.

"That's why we've got these paper forms," she said. "It's a whole new system for most of us, and it takes forever. I know it's hard on the families too."

Finally, Mr. O'Hara was assigned to the intensive care unit—the ICU—on the fifth floor. Mrs. Brown went with him on a special elevator for patients. On the regular elevator, Maura and Luis found a sign taped up: USE STAIRS IF POSSIBLE.

"Five floors?" Luis complained.

"It'll be good for us," Maura said—but she didn't look like she meant it.

The stairwell was crowded and dark. Luis stayed to the right and kept his palm on the railing for guidance. On the fourth-floor landing an overweight man leaned against the wall, wheezing and sweating.

"Are you okay?" Maura asked him.

"Just gotta get my breath," the man panted. "Thanks."

Luis had never thought of climbing stairs as dangerous

before, but what if that guy had a heart attack? Had there even been tall buildings before there were elevators? Luis figured maybe not.

Luis and Maura were both out of breath when at last they made it to the fifth floor. Mrs. Brown was there already, sitting in the ICU waiting area. Her eyes were closed, and she was leaning her head against the wall behind her.

"Mom?" Maura said. "Resting your eyes?"

"Exactly," Mrs. Brown said.

"Have you talked to the doctor? What did he say?" Maura asked.

"It's a she, actually, and your grandpa has had a stroke." Mrs. Brown opened her eyes. "They're going to do a CT scan as soon as they can and give him medicine. They need to find out what part of the brain is affected."

"I know that word—stroke—but I don't really know what it means," Luis said.

"It means a problem with the way your blood flows in your brain," said Mrs. Brown. "Maybe there's a clot, like a scab only on the inside. Maybe a blood vessel broke. Either way, it causes damage. The question is how much."

"Is that why Grandpa's face was all funny?" Maura said. "Is that why he couldn't talk?"

Mrs. Brown shut her eyes again and nodded. "It could be. The affected part might be the part in charge of speech."

"But will he be okay?" Luis asked. This seemed like the important question. Cut to the chase.

Mrs. Brown shrugged one shoulder. "They've already done some tests and given him medicine. The nurse told me people sometimes recover fully, but it depends. Right now he's resting."

"Can we see him?" Maura asked.

"He was awake when I came out here," said Mrs. Brown. "The nurses were fussing with something, so I gave them some space. They'll be gone by now, so go ahead if you want. Oh, wait." She leaned forward and got to her feet slowly. Her eyes were still red, and her face looked pale. "I think I have to go with you. Kids aren't allowed on their own in the ICU."

Luis and Maura followed Mrs. Brown through the double doors. Inside, half a dozen people wearing scrubs stood behind a counter as tall as Luis's chest. All of them were writing on clipboards, talking on the phone, or both.

"The worst part is no coffee," one of them said.

"These are Mr. O'Hara's grandchildren," Mrs. Brown said.

"Don't stay too long," said the woman who was seated. She did not look up.

The ICU was about half the size of the Dudley gymnasium. Lining the walls were hospital beds, each one set off by curtains. Most of the beds were occupied, and all were surrounded by equipment—bags of liquid on poles, beeping heart monitors, wires everywhere. The patients seemed to be part machine themselves.

Unlike the corridor, the ICU was brightly lit. *This is how hospitals are supposed to look,* Luis thought. *Finally, I'm in a room full of normal.*

Mr. O'Hara's color had not improved. When Maura saw him, she blinked and wiped her eyes. Luis said a little prayer to Jesus: *Please, whatever happens, don't ever let me look as bad as that.*

"Grandpa?" Maura said. "It's Maura. My friend Luis is here. The ambulance brought you, remember? Everything is going to be fine."

Luis said a second prayer: *One more thing, Jesus. Please never again let anyone talk to me in a preschool-teacher voice.*

Suddenly—spookily—Mr. O'Hara's right eye opened wide, or maybe it only looked wide compared to the collapsed left side of his face. The eyeball darted around as if seeking someplace to focus. *He looks scared,* Luis thought, and then Luis felt scared himself.

Mr. O'Hara opened his mouth, closed it, then mumbled something that seemed to be nonsense. "Zap," he said, and then, "Seven forty-two."

CHAPTER TEN

Mrs. Brown hadn't understood what her father said. Maura repeated it, and she shrugged. "According to the doctor, they babble sometimes. It's like the signal between the brain and the tongue is bad."

"Didn't he say it before, though?" Luis asked Maura. "Zap."

Maura didn't answer. Mr. O'Hara had closed his eyes again. Now he looked more peaceful. *Maybe he was delivering a message,* Luis thought. *He said it, and now he feels better. But what does the message mean?*

"I think we can go home, kiddo," Mrs. Brown said to her daughter. "It's been quite a day, and I am beat and starving. How about a can of cold chili for dinner? *Mmm*—doesn't that sound good?"

Maura told her grandpa good-bye, and the three of them made their way back through the ICU.

"You're forgetting, Mom," Maura said. "We've got a camp stove. We can heat up chili—and tea and hot chocolate too."

In the corridor, Mrs. Brown blinked. "I did forget," she said.

"Maybe we should invite neighbors over?" Maura said. "Luis, do you want to come? Other people aren't as lucky as us, after all. They are going to be hungry for something warm."

"Luis is always welcome," Mrs. Brown said. "The power will be back soon, but if it's not . . ."

"What?" Maura looked at her mom.

Mrs. Brown shrugged. "If it's not, we might need those supplies for ourselves. The neighbors will be fine. No one's going to starve."

"Hot food sounds great, thanks, but I'm gonna go home," Luis said. "I should see about my parents. For sure their phones are dead."

The TV was still on in the lobby when they walked through after the long descent. "—with alarm systems out of commission, there are scattered reports of looting and vandalism coming in from around . . . ," the news anchor was saying.

Luis had to push hard on the automatic doors to open them. Under the portico outside, a security guard with a flashlight met them. "Walk you to your car, folks?" he said.

"Oh, that won't be necessary, will it?" Mrs. Brown said.

"It's a good idea, ma'am," he said. "Situation like this brings out the worst in some people. With your kids, and all . . ."

Mrs. Brown shrugged. "Okay."

"My bike's right here," Luis told the guard.

"Sure you don't need a ride?" Maura asked. "We can throw the bike in the trunk."

"Actually . . ." Mrs. Brown looked embarrassed. "I'm almost out of gas."

"I gotta make a stop on the way anyway," Luis said. "If any bad guys try to chase me, I'll outrun 'em."

"See you at school tomorrow," Maura said. "At least I hope."

Luis smiled. "Did you ever think you'd say 'I hope' about going to school?"

Luis unlocked his bike and jumped on. Bathed in darkness, the town of Hampton felt unfamiliar, and the ride seemed much longer than it should have. The only light came from the moon, the city across the river, and the few cars out on the road. The darkened fast-food places made the landscape especially weird. McDonald's, Popeyes, and Taco Bell were as much a part of his geography as the river was. With them changed, everything else seemed to be changed too.

Cresting a hill, Luis briefly viewed a black ribbon of water and the tall buildings of the big, brightly lit city beyond. In English at the end of last year, they had learned about metaphor. A metaphor was when you used one thing to stand in for another, like calling sadness a dark sea, or a fast-moving football a bullet. Now it seemed to Luis as if the bright city and the dark city were metaphors—one for hope and the other for despair.

The stop Luis wanted to make was at Señora Álvaro's bodega. He'd been hauling around the chocolate milk all day in his backpack. What were the odds that it was still okay to drink? Anyway, he had to fess up that he'd never found the genius. He'd go looking tomorrow, he'd promise. He hoped she was still there. He hoped she wouldn't be too mad.

Two blocks from the bodega, Luis saw shadows moving in the vacant lot on Erie Street. As he watched, they morphed into three slender figures—kids, teenagers probably. Luis's mental map of the neighborhood had been earned by thorough exploration. They must have come through the rickety fence from the alley. Luis swung his bike left onto Main Street. Halfway down the block, he could make out the bodega on the corner. It was dark like everywhere. Had Señora Álvaro given up in the dark? But wait, something flickered inside. A candle maybe, or a lantern. Like Maura's grandpa, Señora Álvaro must have been prepared for a blackout. If Luis had to bet, he would bet she was in there counting up cash.

Señora Álvaro was meticulous that way. "Meticulous" was one of her words, meaning careful to do things right. She always said que no era Einstein—she was no Einstein—but she was meticulous. That was how she kept her bodega in business. Meticulous and tough.

Without bothering to brake, Luis threw his leg over his bike seat, jumped off, and ran alongside till the front tire bumped the door.

"¡Hola, Señora! Hey, it's me, Luis!"

"Dios mío. Un momentito," Señora Álvaro said. "¿Qué quieres, Luis? How has the dark day treated you? One thing good, for once I go to bed early. Tú también. Take my advice. No watching videos on your phone. Save the battery!"

"Claro, Señora, por supuesto," he answered, and then he hesitated. He didn't really want to confess. He'd put it off a second or two. "Are you okay here by yourself? I saw some kids around, and I heard on TV there's been trouble—people stealing from stores, I guess."

Señora Álvaro shook her head. "My neighbors would never mess with la señora. If I close up, where do they get their cigarettes and Red Bull?"

"Bueno, bueno—" Luis was getting ready to say why he'd stopped by when a *crack* interrupted. This was followed by the sound of shattering glass, then sharp voices, and a squeal of laughter—all of it much too close. It sounded like a window smashed in the storeroom behind the bodega.

Luis felt a pang and straightened up. He wasn't so much afraid as he was ready: *If you're coming in, let's do this already.*

"Dios mío," Señora Álvaro murmured, and Luis thought he saw her cross herself. "Don't you—," she started to tell him, perhaps remembering the kid setting himself up to protect her was all of eleven years old.

Luis wished his brother were there. He wished there was only one kid instead of three. He even wished—halfway—that he had ridden on by Señora Álvaro's bodega so that he was home now, bored maybe, but safe in his own blue room.

He hadn't, though. And he'd known Señora Álvaro all his life. She needed his help. Unconsciously, he squared his shoulders.

"Hey, you kids!" He tried to make his voice deep and scary. "You get outta here before we call the police."

More sharp voices. More laughter. Then a *crack* like a stick hitting the metal siding of the store. A stick, or a baseball bat? Luis didn't like to think of baseball bats. Did they have a gun? Señora Álvaro had always bragged she didn't need one. Like she said, the neighborhood needed her bodega and would protect it.

So tonight I am the neighborhood, Luis thought.

The sounds seemed to be moving from the back of the bodega toward the front. Maybe breaking a window, making noise—it was just somebody's idea of entertainment. Or were they coming inside?

Luis got his answer a moment later when the front door pushed open, and the shadows became all too solid flesh and blood.

"You kids get out of here!" Señora Álvaro puffed up with courage. "What would your parents—"

"You been taking in cash all day, right, Señora? It's only right you should share," said the tallest of the shadows—a boy with a red ski mask covering his face.

"Share and share alike," said a girl, "you know, same as Sunday school."

She was about Luis's height but had a very grown-up shape. She wasn't masked, but Luis didn't know her. She must not live in the neighborhood. Maybe the tall kid was trying to impress her?

The third kid, a boy also without a mask, began to laugh uncontrollably. He was unsteady on his feet. He leaned against the freezer case and hiccupped.

"Share and share alike," the girl repeated. She must've liked the way that sounded. Now Luis realized the two of them were drunk. The odor of tequila breath filled the small space.

"Get outta here," Luis repeated. "Get outta here now. The señora is my friend."

"If she's so friendly, she wants to help us out, right?" said the tall boy, who was crazy if he thought the mask disguised him. His name was Tony Cencerro, and everyone knew he bossed a loose band of kids who were in and out of trouble for stupid petty crimes. Bad as he was, Tony disliked guns. That was one reason a lot of parents turned a blind eye if their kids ran with him. The parents hoped it would keep their kids out of worse trouble, more dangerous gangs.

The drunk boy began to moan. "I don't feel so good."

Tony looked down at him, disgusted. "Entonces, go on home to Mamita."

Luis began to calculate. *Tony's around sixteen, I think. I can take him if I have to. I can take him because I'm smarter. Also, I haven't been drinking. No problem.*

An opposing voice spoke in Luis's head, too, a sane one, his brother's maybe, and it said: *What are you talking about? You're eleven. You are half his size. All those push-ups won't count for much against his weight advantage. You are going to get annihilated. Run while you can!*

"I called the cops. They're are on their way," Señora Álvaro lied.

"The police got emergencies all over South Jersey," Tony said. "They'll get here next week if you're lucky."

With that Tony advanced toward the counter.

And Luis sidestepped to face him.

"What're you, the Karate Kid?" Tony grabbed Luis's shoulder, ready to shove him aside. But Luis set his feet and clenched his right fist. Annihilated maybe, but he'd get in one punch, and he would give it all he had.

But then Jesus, or someone, stepped in to help him out. From the vicinity of the drunk kid, who should've gone home to his mamita when he had the chance, came the unmistakable sound of puking—followed at once by the unmistakable smell.

"Are you kidding me?" Distracted, Tony looked over his shoulder at the still retching boy. Seeing his chance, Luis let go with a right that knocked Tony off-balance, followed by a left that knocked him into the candy rack. "*Ow*—hey!" Tony put up his hand and lurched forward so that his left foot skidded into the vomit and he sat down hard.

The girl, meanwhile, was shrieking. Laughing? Crying? Luis couldn't tell.

Tony seemed to be paralyzed for the moment, still trying to figure out what had happened. One second he'd been on his feet about to grab some cash, and the next he was on the floor, his butt soaking in vomit.

Soon the sick boy stumbled to the door to leave. The girl—sulking now—was right behind him.

"Vaya con Dios," Luis said.

"Tú también—you too." Señora Álvaro nodded at Tony.

A minute passed before the masked boy accepted the inevitable, got to his feet, and made for the door—his jeans filthy, wet, and reeking. You could almost feel sorry for him, Luis thought. Almost but not quite.

"I'll be back," he said, and pulled the door closed.

"Tontos," Señora Álvaro said. Now that the danger was over, she seemed to shrink back to her usual size. Her voice had a quaver in it too. All that courage had been for show, Luis thought, or maybe courage was always for show. "¡Ay, qué lástima!" she went on.

"I'll clean it up," said Luis. "I'm used to it."

"What do you mean?" Señora Álvaro asked.

Shoot. Luis hadn't meant to say it out loud. "Nada, never mind. Where's the mop?"

The truth was he was used to cleaning up after his parents, who often bragged that they partied as hard as they worked. They weren't even embarrassed when they got sick. It was part of the deal. They were entitled. And as for the kid cleaning it up, someday his kids would do the same for him. That was the way they saw it, the way the world worked.

But Luis had sworn no way.

His kids would never have to do that, would never see him drunk or hungover either. His kids would think he was the perfect dad, the perfect person, because he would try to be. They were going to live in a house like Maura's— *nicer* than Maura's—have the kind of life he saw on TV.

Señora Álvaro argued a little and then handed over a mop. Luis knew she wasn't going to thank him, either for stepping up to protect her or for cleaning up. Like Luis's parents, she would accept his services as something kids owed grown-ups.

Then—unexpectedly—she handed over something besides the mop, a big responsibility.

"I hate to say it, but those kids were right," she told him as he finished up. "I do have a lot of cash with nowhere to go till the bank is open again. Will you keep it for me?"

"Keep money?" Luis could not believe his ears.

"No one thinks a kid has money." Señora Álvaro shrugged. "If those punks tried to take it from me, others will too. I don't want to stay here all night on guard duty, and I don't want it upstairs in my apartment either. Too many people know I live alone. With you—with your family—it will be safe."

"How much is it?" Luis asked.

"More than a thousand," Señora Álvaro said. "Something about emergencies makes people stuff their cupboards. There's probably not a paper towel or a can of soup between here and Nueva York. One guy bought all my orange juice. Why did he need so much orange juice?"

Luis wasn't sure about taking so much money. The idea scared him a little, but at the same time, Señora Álvaro's trust made him feel important, like a big man.

At last he said okay, and the señora handed over a metal box. She had just finished counting when the shadow trio invaded. She admitted to Luis that now that the danger was past, she felt a little shaky.

"I'll keep it safe, Señora, I promise." Luis opened his backpack to put in the box and saw the carton of milk. If he told her about Computer Genius now, she couldn't be mad, could she? Not after all that had happened. He started to explain, but the señora wasn't listening.

"Thank you, Mijo. I'm going to bed," she said. "By the way, I know exactly how much I am giving you. And I know I'll get every centavo back."

CHAPTER ELEVEN

L uis found his bike where he'd left it. *Thank you, Jesus,* he thought. *Or maybe thank the tequila gods this time.* Tony and the others must have known the bike was his, but they had felt too sick or too gross to take the time for revenge.

Luis pedaled quickly through the darkness, keenly aware of the extra weight in his backpack. *More than a thousand dollars,* he thought. *I won't let the señora down.*

Then he remembered he'd already let her down by failing to find Computer Genius. *I'll do that tomorrow,* he thought. *I'll deliver the chocolate milk too.*

Like Maura earlier, Luis flipped the light switch as soon as he walked in the front door. *Estúpido,* he thought when—of course—nothing happened. Since he couldn't see anyway, he closed his eyes. It made no difference and felt more comfortable.

"¿Hola?" he called, but no one answered. He imagined

his parents drinking at a bar in the dark. Would the beer taps work? They might miss the TVs or the noise of the jukebox, but in the end it was the beer that mattered.

Pushing his bike with one hand, Luis felt his way through the room, bumping furniture as he went. *Everybody in Hampton probably has bruised shins by now,* he thought. *That's the number they should put on the news— two hundred thousand customers without power, four hundred thousand bruised shins.*

In his room, Luis felt for the hook on the wall and hung up his bike. Then he dropped his backpack onto his bed, felt his way into the bathroom, and learned that the house still had water pressure.

When finally he lay down, he realized he was feeling shaky, not scared exactly, more like uncomfortable with all the darkness and uncertainty. Knowing the power could come back any second almost made him feel worse. He thought of Tony on the floor of Señora Álvaro's bodega—one moment ready to grab a wad of money from an old woman, the next crawling out the door, smelly and empty-handed. It was always true, Luis guessed, but the power outage had made it real: Your world could flip over in an instant.

With all that on his mind—and a thousand dollars in

his backpack at the foot of his bed—Luis shouldn't have been able to sleep. But sleep he did. At some point his parents came in noisily. For sure, their shins could be counted among the bruised. Luis registered the noise, rolled over, and returned to his dreams.

When he awoke for good, the sky was gray, not black, and the stars were gone. It was morning, right around six o'clock. After so many years, he didn't really need an alarm.

He knew right away the power was still out because the house was freezing. Just to be sure, he checked the clock on his nightstand. It was a round, old-fashioned clock, the kind with hands, and it was stuck at twenty to eight.

Three-two-one—Luis vaulted up. Getting dressed, he thought of something—the time on the microwave clock the day before when it flashed and went black. He tied his shoes and then turned around and looked more closely at the clock on the nightstand. To be precise, it read eighteen minutes before eight—7:42. Wasn't that the number Mr. O'Hara had said at the hospital?

It had to be a coincidence.

But what were the odds of such a coincidence?

Luis was pretty good at math. He had convinced

Reynaldo to stop playing the lottery by calculating that the odds of his winning were much less than the odds of his being bitten by a shark at the shore.

Figuring this out should be simple.

The odds that somebody would say one number rather than another number—that must be like infinity to one, right? There was an infinite number of numbers.

But if Mr. O'Hara had been thinking of a time of day, that made the odds better.

Luis splashed his face with water and thought: *There are sixty times of day every hour, and twenty-four hours in a day—so there must be sixty times twenty-four possible times of day. That makes*—Luis did the multiplication in his head—*one thousand four hundred and forty.*

On the other hand—Luis patted his face dry—*unless you're in the army, you probably think about times of day as one through twelve, not one through twenty-four. So that makes half as many possibilities, seven hundred twenty.*

So the odds of Mr. O'Hara saying the exact time when the power went out were one in seven hundred twenty. That made it more likely than winning the lottery, but still pretty unlikely.

So did that mean there had to be a connection between the blackout and Mr. O'Hara?

Luis shook his head. *This is where math takes you,* he thought, *straight to insanity.* Because—*duh*—the only connection between Mr. O'Hara and the blackout was that Mr. O'Hara used to work for NJL. So did a whole lot of people, right? Maura's mom worked there now. And it was crazy to think she had anything to do with the blackout.

Luis decided to file crazy away for later. Right now he had other problems. Like how he had no idea what was going on with his friends or anyone else. His phone had died in the night. No Facebook, no Snapchat, no Instagram. No texting or e-mail even. It was Ground Control to Major Tom—and Ground Control was AWOL.

Alone in the universe, Luis decided to start with the easy stuff. He removed the box of money from his backpack and slid it under his bed. It would be safe there among the dust bunnies. They hadn't been disturbed since the day he took over the bedroom.

In the kitchen he found one last Pop-Tart and ate it in two bites. He was still hungry, but not hungry enough for his other option, raw oatmeal. Maybe there was still food for sale somewhere in Hampton, or maybe he'd go back to

Maura's. Even canned chili sounded pretty good about now.

Next was to find out about school, and the only way to do that was to bike over there.

For a Tuesday, the streets were quiet. No stores were open. No one seemed to be going to work. Maybe people were saving the gas in their tanks for the real emergency—whatever and whenever that might be.

By the time he got to school, he knew what he would find: The gate closed with a NO SCHOOL TODAY sign posted on it. Below that was an additional note that read: CHECK TV, RADIO, WEB FOR DETAILS. SORRY FOR THE INCONVENIENCE. The information was repeated in Spanish.

Luis thought the sign should have said: HOORAY! ANOTHER DAY OFF! But the dozen or so parents standing there didn't look happy. Did they see it as another day when their kids wouldn't learn anything?

Also, how was anybody supposed to check TV, radio, Web? Phones, tablets, laptops—they must all be dead by now.

Someone punched Luis in the shoulder. Thinking of last night—*Tony*—Luis tensed, instantly on alert. But when he turned around, it was only Carlos. "Hey, Luis, what's shaking?"

"Carlos, my man. Only me—it's freezing at my house. Other than that, not much. How 'bout you?"

"No mucho. I have never slept so much in my life as I did yesterday. Without video games, what's a homie supposed to do?"

"Search me, hue."

"Well, what did you do?"

Luis shrugged. "Nothing. This and that."

"Did you go to Maura's new house? Is it nice?" Carlos asked.

Luis dodged the question. "I been there before. It's got a yard and new carpets."

"Ohhhhh," said Carlos. "You been there before? I see how it is with the two of you."

"Get off my case, Carlos," said Luis.

Carlos started to say something else, but Luis made his fierce face and Carlos changed his mind. "So anyway," Carlos said. "It's official. We have nothing to do today. Trouble is, I don't think I can sleep anymore. I don't think it's humanly possible."

"Señora Álvaro wants me to check on the genius," Luis said. "We could go exploring."

"Exploring" meant exploring abandoned houses. It

was absolutely forbidden by every Hampton parent, and it was every kid's favorite activity.

"Not without light," Carlos said. "Too much garbage in those houses. Too many needles. Do you have any idea what kinds of diseases you get from those needles?"

Luis shrugged. "So I'll get us light, then."

"Isn't your phone dead?" Carlos asked. "My parents have a flashlight but no batteries. Do you think anybody's got batteries?"

"No," said Luis. "But I have an idea."

Carlos raised his eyebrows. "Does your idea got something to do with Maura?"

Luis flashed the fierce face again.

"Sheesh, you are touchy on certain subjects," Carlos said.

Luis ignored this. "Come with me if you got nothing to do. I bet I know somebody who could use your help. Later, I'll get us some light."

CHAPTER TWELVE

Luis's idea did have something to do with Maura. She—or more accurately, her family's hall closet—was going to provide him with a flashlight. Meanwhile, Carlos could keep busy helping Señora Álvaro out in her bodega.

In Luis's mind, Carlos would be helping to repay the señora for Luis's failing to find the genius the day before. Luis knew that didn't exactly make sense. After all, Carlos hadn't let the señora down—he had. Still, Carlos was his friend with nothing else to do. He might as well be useful.

At the bodega, the sign on the door read OPEN—CASH ONLY with a new line at the bottom: OWNER IS ARMED.

Inside the small dark space, half a dozen shoppers milled around the almost empty shelves. Luis was glad about one thing. The smell of so many people this early in the morning obliterated the smell of vomit from the night before.

The señora was behind the counter selling her last bottle of Palmolive to a regular customer. Luis nodded at her, then hung back waiting for a chance to speak without the whole neighborhood overhearing.

Finally, he moved toward her. "Señora, are you really armed?" he asked quietly.

"Tal vez—maybe." She shrugged. "I gotta say it on my sign, though, in case Tony or one of his friends comes back."

"Wait—you recognized him?" Luis said.

"I'm old. I'm not blind," said Señora Álvaro.

"Do you want me to bring back your money?" Luis asked. "Now that it's daylight, I mean?"

Señora Álvaro looked to see no one was listening and then shook her head. "Your house is better than a bank, Luis. And I don't want to have to prove how tough I am—you get what I'm saying? What if I hurt somebody?"

Luis smiled. "Yeah, I get it."

"Hey, good people, have you heard?" Mrs. Freeman, a tall African-American woman, came through the door from the sidewalk, waving her arms. "They're calling in the United States Armed Forces!"

"Oh, sí?" Señora Álvaro said calmly.

"Unh-hunh. It was all over the television last night. My sister from Raleigh told me. Tanks and bombs and I don't know what else."

"Why would they want to do that?" Señora Álvaro asked.

"On account of the looters and rioters and *killers*! Have you been over on Spruce Street this morning? Looks like somebody dropped a bomb! So therefore—*boom*—the president is going to teach them a lesson."

"It's Communists that are responsible. That's what I heard." This comment came from a short man with white hair who was wearing green sweatpants.

"Which Communists?" Señora Álvaro asked.

"The North Koreans, I bet," said a white guy with a goatee. "They've got nukes, plus their government is known to be crazy."

"Why would somebody way over there in North Korea care about you and me and Hampton, New Jersey?" Señora Álvaro asked.

"We're the test case. After us, they take out New York City." The guy spoke as if this were totally obvious.

Mrs. Freeman was nodding. "That's what my sister says the president claimed on the television. It could be we fight back against them and *boom!* World War III!"

"And it could be the wind knocked down a power line," said a gray-haired tía in a dress with a floral pattern. She wore glasses and orthopedic shoes.

"The wind nothing! I am quoting no less than the president of the *United States*," Mrs. Freeman said. "But not to worry. Our armed forces can fix the Communists—*boom!*"

"*Ay.*" Señora Álvaro rubbed her head with her palm. "So you're saying the Communists and the looters are the same now, Maddie?"

Mrs. Freeman raised her eyebrows and nodded. "Could be. Working together. A *conspiracy.*"

"Did anybody hear that Julia lady that's running for mayor? The one that makes babies cry?" the guy with the goatee asked. "She says it's corporations and government that turned off the power to keep the common people down. She said we oughta go out in the street and demand our rights."

"Seguro, she said that," Señora Álvaro said. "She wants to blame everything on the guy in charge of the city, on Mayor Manuel."

"Excuse me, Señora?" A man Luis recognized from the tire bodega had opened the door and leaned in. "You got any phone batteries?"

"I wish I did," Señora Álvaro said. "I could sell a million."

"You know anybody that does?" the guy asked.

Señora Álvaro shook her head.

"My cousin's son-in-law's buddy said he's gonna drive to North Jersey and buy up a supply and come back. I bet he makes a ton of money," said the man with the goatee.

"I heard people are buying cans of gas and charging fifty bucks a gallon," Mrs. Freeman said. "They're doing it with other stuff too—potato chips, Gatorade, you know, necessities."

Señora Álvaro scoffed. "You make money till the power's back. Then you got too much inventory and you lose money," she said.

"Honey, haven't you been paying attention?" Mrs. Freeman said. "The power is not coming back. This is not what you call *normal*. This is some kind of war against the people that'll only get worse, then—*boom!*"

Luis did not know what to think about all this talk. There were people in the bodega rolling their eyes at Mrs. Freeman and other people listening and shaking their heads. Señora Álvaro seemed skeptical.

Carlos bumped Luis's arm. "What are we doing here anyway, hue?"

"Oh yeah, right," Luis said. "Here is the plan. You stay and help Señora Álvaro while I go take care of my, uh . . . business."

Carlos shrugged. "Could be that's cool," he said, "depending on the hourly?"

"The hourly you have to work out with the señora. Maybe hourly gratitude and appreciation."

"Say what? I don't work for appreciation," said Carlos. "I gotta have dinero, you know, an *hourly.*"

"Gimme a break, Carlos. Like otherwise you've got so many responsibilities to attend to? You told me you were sick of sleeping. Here, provided by me, is an alternative activity. Maybe if the señora has anything left such as chips or soda or candy, she might give you some, capeesh?"

"What is this capeesh of which you speak?" Carlos asked.

"Do you un-der-stand?" Luis emphasized each sylla-ble.

"I un-der-stand," said Carlos. "Señora"—he turned to her—"looks like you got yourself a helper."

Señora Álvaro looked Carlos up and down, then pursed her lips. "I guess I can find something for you to do."

Back outdoors on the sidewalk, Luis heard a familiar

sound—the loudspeaker-distorted voice of Julia Girardo: "We all remember a time when Hampton was a great city!" she shouted. "A time when manufacturing jobs made this a great place to live! But look at it now. Families who can afford to have moved away, leaving empty houses, gangs, and crime behind. *You*, the victims of a rigged system, ought to rise up and reclaim what's yours! My mission is to help. Do you have questions? I have all the answers!"

The day before, Luis and Maura had been the only ones on the sidewalk when Julia Girardo rolled by. But now there was applause and even cheering. *People must be bored like Carlos*, Luis thought. *Julia Girardo is the closest thing to a parade.*

On his way to Maura's, Luis made a quick stop at home.

His dad was awake and thumping around the kitchen in search of breakfast. Still sleepy, he tapped switches on the microwave, the lights, the stove—and cursed one thing after another when it didn't work.

"You know the power's out, right?" Luis said. "It's been out since yesterday morning?"

"Of course I know," his father said. "You think I'm a moron or something?"

"I do not think you're a moron," Luis said.

"¡Verdad!" Luis's father thumped the kitchen counter with his fist and looked around the darkened room. "How is a person supposed to live like this anyway? It's . . . it's *primitive!* What about the diner, Luis? Do you know if it's open?"

"Nobody's got power," Luis said. "There's all kinds of rumors, but nobody seems to know when it will be back."

Luis's dad opened the refrigerator and made a face. "Smells bad in there," he said.

"It would help if we cleaned it sometimes," Luis said.

"It doesn't matter if you clean it when it's cold and the smells are frozen," his dad said.

"You could clean it now," Luis said. "You're not going to work, are you? Is work happening?"

"¿Quién sabe? Who knows? Does Señora Álvaro have any food at her bodega? I need food. Without food for fuel, how is a man supposed to think?"

"I was just there, and I don't think so," Luis said. "If you've got enough gas in the car, you should probably drive to somewhere with power."

"Where is that?" his dad asked.

"Across the river," Luis said. "Or south. Delaware."

Luis's dad shook his head. "I was gonna get gas yesterday. . . ."

Luis's mom appeared in the doorway between his parents' bedroom and the kitchen. "You mean there's no gas at the gas stations?" she asked.

"Pumps don't work without power, Mamá," Luis said.

"I thought they were all supposed to have generators now," his dad said.

"All I know is they're closed," Luis said. He was kind of enjoying this. His parents were drowsy, confused, and grumpy. He, in contrast, was wide-awake and getting used to life during a blackout. Maybe he was a rotten kid for enjoying his parents' frustration, but if so, okay. He was a rotten kid.

"So I gotta go," he said.

"¿Dónde?" His dad turned on him and scowled. He was twenty years older than Luis's mom—old enough to be an abuelo, a grandfather. He had thin white hair and a fleshy face that in old photos was angular like Luis's. Luis's older brother, Reynaldo, was technically his half brother, born to a different mother. She lived in Nicaragua. Luis's dad and his mom had met working at a restaurant in Juarez, Mexico, during the long trip north from Central America.

"To Maura's house," Luis said. He hated revealing anything to his parents, but in this case the truth was easier than a lie. They wouldn't try to stop his going to Maura's, and since his phone was dead, they couldn't reel him back either.

"Me gusta esa chica Maura. I like her," said his mother. She was still young with a nice shape, something Luis knew but didn't like knowing, something his brother's friends frequently commented on. In fact, she was only five years older than Luis's brother. Her hair was straight and black but currently uncombed. She spent a lot of time on her skin and eyebrows; just now the effect was spoiled by smudged makeup.

Luis's mom worked hard and partied hard, same as Luis's dad, but she could be sweet too. When Luis was little, she had sung him lullabies. Now, when he was sad or couldn't fall asleep, he thought of her singing. He had never told that to anyone.

"Yeah, I do, too, I guess," he said. "Me tengo que ir— gotta go. And buena suerte con el desayuno."

CHAPTER THIRTEEN

Luis was going to Maura's for three reasons:

1. Get something to eat, maybe even something hot.

2. Ask about the mystery of 742. Had Maura heard the number the same way Luis did?

3. Score flashlight batteries.

When that was done, he and Carlos could go find Computer Genius and make sure he was okay, maybe deliver day-old chocolate milk.

How long did chocolate milk keep, anyway?

Of course, Luis thought, *Computer Genius has to be okay. That is the nature of Computer Genius. The legend requires it.*

Still inside the Hampton city limits, Luis rode down Spruce Street—a block that looters had ransacked. Windows were broken, doors hung loose on their hinges, café tables and chairs lay in ragtag pieces on the street. The police had come and gone—too busy to stick around. Their yellow tape by now had been ripped down to join the broken glass and litter. A few people were going through the mess. Business owners? Scavengers looking for leftovers? Luis couldn't tell.

He rode on. At the mall on the highway, TV trucks had arrived overnight and now formed a small antennaed city in the parking lot. The big satellite trucks were from all over—New York City, Philadelphia, Washington DC, Baltimore, Pittsburgh—too many to count. Farther east was a collection of white trucks with the Red Cross symbol on the side. In front of them were long tables and people in uniforms handing out something—doughnuts maybe? Coffee? Luis thought of stopping—a doughnut sounded great right about now; his stomach was emptier than ever, but the lines were too long. Luis did not have much patience for lines.

Contrary to the rumors in Señora Álvaro's bodega, no United States armed forces were in sight, but there were plenty of police cars on the streets; helicopters hovered overhead.

Luis made the turn off the highway, then the right turn onto Maura's street. Mrs. Brown's car was in the driveway. Luis leaned his bike against the house and pulled out his phone to text Maura before realizing, uh . . . no, he would not be using it to text. Instead, he would have to knock on the door—announce himself old-school. The looted stores, the media city, the cop cars everywhere, and now this.

Without power, so many things were strange.

"Luis, welcome. It's nice to see you," Mrs. Brown said when she opened the door. Her hair was messy, as if she hadn't gotten around to brushing it yet. There were circles under her eyes. She wore yoga pants and a stretched-out T-shirt. Like her father, Mr. O'Hara, Mrs. Brown always looked well dressed and tidy, so her appearance was another strange thing. At least she was as nice as ever. "Are you hungry?" she wanted to know.

Luis nodded. "Yes."

Mrs. Brown smiled, which made her look better. "Come on in and have some oatmeal. Do you like oatmeal? I think we are perfecting our camp-stove cooking skills, Maura and me. She's outside. I'm gonna go ahead and get dressed."

"Okay," said Luis, but when she left he thought of something. *Why is Mrs. Brown home, anyway?* She worked for NJL. He remembered that yesterday her boss had sent her home. But today you'd think all the employees would be on the job. It was an emergency just like a hurricane—right?

Luis's didn't like the next thought that came to him. Could Mrs. Brown have had something to do with the outage? Was she in trouble at work for that?

Luis shook his head. Mrs. Brown was nice. Nice people didn't turn off power to whole cities. It was only a coincidence that her boss had sent her home.

Luis walked through the living room and kitchen, then slid open the glass door that led to the patio. Maura was there, watching over a two-burner gas camp stove, which sputtered on the picnic table. There was a pan on one burner, a tin coffeepot on the other.

Seeing this setup, Luis thought of his mom. When she was a kid in Nicaragua, her family had cooked outdoors. He was pretty sure their stove and pots weren't as shiny and new as Maura's.

"Hey. Good morning. I thought you might show up," Maura said. "I bet you're hungry."

"There's other reasons I'm here." Luis hated her apparent ability to read his mind.

"Name one," said Maura.

"Batteries," Luis said.

"Not because we're friends?" Maura said.

"What? Us?" Luis said. "I guess. How is your grandpa?"

"Okay, I hope. They said they'd send a messenger if anything changed, and nobody's come." Maura took the lid off the pan, spooned oatmeal into a plastic bowl and handed it to Luis. "Sorry if it's gluey. In other news, there's raisins and sugar." She nodded at the table. "And the same little creamers you get at a coffee place."

"Just like camping—I mean, I guess," Luis said. "I've never been camping."

"Me neither," said Maura.

Luis tore the paper off a couple of creamers. "So your family doesn't go camping? I thought that must be why you had all this stuff."

Maura had scooped herself a bowl of oatmeal by this time. She sat down and leaned over the table to get raisins and sugar. "I don't know why we have it actually. It was another one of Grandpa's good ideas." Maura took a bite of oatmeal. "Gluey," she pronounced with her mouth full.

"Aw, it's not that bad," Luis said. "And it's warm. Thank you."

While they ate, Luis told Maura about the gossip at Señora Álvaro's, the looted stores, and the line for Red Cross doughnuts.

"Why do you need batteries so bad?" Maura asked.

"Carlos and I are gonna go find the genius," Luis said. He didn't have to explain who that was. Maura knew. Everybody did. "We need light to go exploring."

"We don't have the rechargeable kind," Maura said. "But we have regular ones for flashlights and lanterns. It's better if we don't tell Mom, though. She's acting weird about our stuff—like the neighbors might go all walking dead and break in. Do you want more oatmeal?"

"Is there enough?" Luis asked. "I wouldn't want to act like the walking dead."

"So long as we're on the same side." Maura was spooning Luis another oatmeal glob when her mom appeared through the glass door. Mrs. Brown now looked clean and awake, but she still had on her yoga pants. When she came out the door, Maura looked up and frowned. "Aren't you going to work?" she asked.

"Not today," Mrs. Brown said. "I guess I'm in trouble."

"You were employee of the month," said Maura.

"Twice," Mrs. Brown said. "But when the blackout

started yesterday, I was on the dispatch board. Everything looked perfectly normal, no alarms. But the boss needed to blame somebody, and I was handy. He sent me home—practically implied the outage was my fault. If he wants me back, he knows where to find me."

Maura shook her head. "You know more about the power company than he does, I bet. You practically grew up at NJL."

"Maybe so," Mrs. Brown said, "but I'm not the one in charge."

"What do you think caused the blackout, Mrs. Brown?" Luis asked. "There's all kinds of crazy rumors around. People are saying the power won't come back at all."

Mrs. Brown shrugged. "I don't want to contribute to the rumors. What are they saying on the news, Maura?"

"I turned it off after I heard it a hundred times," Maura said. "Mostly they just repeat that they don't know either. Yesterday they were telling people to stay home—shelter in place—but it changed this morning. Now the Red Cross is setting up shelters in Mount Laurel and Voorhees. If it goes on past tomorrow, then something called fee-ma comes."

"That's FEMA—the Federal Emergency Management Agency," Mrs. Brown said.

Maura nodded. "Okay. Besides that, people are getting hurt. Someone could die."

"Mrs. Brown," Luis said, "can I ask another question—a dumb question?"

Mrs. Brown shrugged. "Sure. It looks like I've got all day."

"What is the board you told us about, the one you look at in your job? I mean, I know it's equipment, but equipment that does what exactly?"

Mrs. Brown ran her hand through her hair and took a breath, like she would need a lot of air to get through this explanation. For a second Luis was sorry he had asked. Maybe the whole electricity deal would be hard for him to understand? But he was smart, wasn't he? Smart anytime he tried to be.

"Let's start basic," Mrs. Brown said. "You know there are three power grids in the continental United States, right? East, west, and Texas?"

"Did not know that," Luis said.

"Most people don't, Mom," Maura said. "Most people only know you plug a plug into the wall and the hair dryer works. Or, like today, doesn't work."

Mrs. Brown drummed her fingers on the table. "Okay,

let's try this. Electricity is generated at power plants in various places, right? There's a dam south of here called Conowingo, and water flowing through it turns turbines that generate electricity. There's a plant down the shore called Oyster Creek, where nuclear reactions heat up water that makes steam—same deal. In Ohio and Indiana, it's mostly coal-fired plants. There are half a dozen natural gas plants in New Jersey. In windy places, you have wind turbines. Except for solar, almost all power plants are based on turbines. The turbines spin a generator, and the generator makes electricity."

"Turbines are like fans, right?" Luis asked.

"Right. The turbine spins a metal wire—a conductor—between the positive and negative poles of a magnet. The magnetic action gets electrons in the wire moving—in other words creates a current. It's easier to step up the voltage for transmission and then step it down for delivery, so alternating current—AC—is usually what's in the lines."

"Do you know what 'alternating current' means?" Maura asked.

"Nope," Luis said.

"It means the current reverses direction instead of

flowing one way," she explained. "When it flows one way, it's direct current—DC."

Luis wasn't sure he had understood all that. He was a little unclear about what voltage meant and how it related to current too. Also, if solar power didn't work with turbines, how did it work? Luis wanted to ask more questions, but he had the feeling he already was processing as much information as was humanly possible in one morning. "Turbines," he repeated. "Magnet. AC. DC. Got it. But how does the grid work? It seems like it ought to be simple—generate power here, and send it there."

"I guess it would be except for one thing," Mrs. Brown said. "Nobody has ever invented a cheap, efficient way to store lots of electricity. For that reason, the amount in the system, in the grid, has to balance with the amount being used. If it doesn't—if there's too much here or too little there—equipment gets fried, lines sag and start fires, outages happen, bad stuff."

"So if it's all connected up," Luis said, "does a tree falling on a power line in Texas shut down a toaster in New York City?"

Mrs. Brown smiled. "Luckily, no. But one reason it doesn't is that somebody is paying attention. With all the factors involved—half a million miles of power line, three thousand utility companies, thousands of power plants, zillions of toasters and hair dryers—powerful computers have to keep watch. My job is to help the computers out, monitor what they're doing, shift the flow of electricity around, make sure supply and demand stay very close to equal."

"Is that that SCADA thing you talk about?" Maura asked.

Mrs. Brown nodded. "SCADA is a system: 'supervisory control and data acquisition.' Basically, the SCADA runs the grid, and dispatchers like me watch over the SCADA."

"What does SCADA do if the system gets out of balance?" Luis asked.

"It can tell the power plant to generate less power," said Mrs. Brown. "It can use relays to shift power from one place to another. In an emergency, it disconnects a problem circuit from the system. That's what must've happened here in Hampton, why the outage doesn't just keep growing. Circuit breakers isolated the problem to contain it."

This was all pretty interesting. But none of it answered the basic question. What caused the blackout? An accident? Foreign enemies? Some random bad guy?

And whoever it was—why?

Luis had never played detective before, but now he wondered if there might be a way for him to find the answers. Computers might be part of it—that SCADA thing. And if the solution involved computers, he knew just the place to start.

CHAPTER FOURTEEN

Mrs. Brown sat up straight and looked in the direction of town and Whitman Hospital. "What I wouldn't give for a powered-up phone," she said.

"You're worried about Grandpa," Maura said.

Mrs. Brown nodded. She had eaten only half her oatmeal, Luis noticed. She had been talking. That was one reason. But he would bet her stomach was knotted up too.

"Luis and I can bike over if you want," Maura volunteered.

"Uh . . . I have to be somewhere," Luis said.

Maura lifted one shoulder. "Then I guess I'll go myself, Mom. No big deal."

Mrs. Brown made a face. "Not sure I like that idea, honey. But if Luis is busy . . ."

Now Luis felt terrible. Even apart from getting breakfast and batteries, he ought to help his friend's family, right? It was the good thing to do. "It's okay. I can go with Maura," he told Mrs. Brown. "I'll meet up with Carlos later."

"Thanks," Maura said.

"I'm not sure how helpful I'm going to be, though," Luis said. "So we're at the hospital, and then what? We send a bird back with a note for your mom?"

"A carrier pigeon," Maura said. "Or what about Pony Express?"

"Morse code?" Luis said. "And are smoke signals a real thing? I've never been sure."

Suddenly, Maura's eyebrows shot up. "Wait a second," she said. "I know where there's a phone."

"What do you mean? A phone that isn't dead?" her mom asked.

Maura nodded toward the garage. "Grandpa's. Usually he keeps it plugged in and turned off. You know how he believes in 'saving the battery.'"

"How did we forget that?" her mom said. "But one phone's no help, honey. We need two."

Maura stood up. "You keep Grandpa's phone. We'll find one at the hospital to call from. Come on, Luis. Let's go get it."

Luis didn't like Maura ordering him around. On the other hand, his fingers were itching for a phone—even one that wasn't his own. He hadn't been without one for this many hours since he was little. It wasn't exactly as bad as losing a hand—or maybe it was.

No one had been in Mr. O'Hara's apartment since the EMTs took him out, and the place was a mess—furniture shoved out of place, magazines and papers on the floor, a potted plant tipped over, scuff marks on the carpet.

"We'll clean it up later," Maura said, "before he comes home. There's the phone on the windowsill like always." In an instant it was in her hand, and she was powering it up. Luis looked at the screen, willing the white icon to appear. It did, and then the battery indicator too. The phone was almost fully charged.

"This ought to last us till the power comes back, right?" Maura said.

"Hope so," said Luis, but then the "enter pass code" screen appeared.

"Shoot!" Maura said. "I hadn't thought of that."

"I heard somewhere it's always one-two-three-four," Luis said, "since most people aren't creative."

Maura tried, but that wasn't it. She looked at Luis.

"We can't make too many mistakes, or it will think we're hackers and lock us out."

"Numbers of his favorite football players?" Luis said.

"I hope not," Maura said. "Because I have no idea who that is. Besides, even though he watches, he thinks criminals fix the games so a particular team wins and the criminals make money."

Luis shook his head. "So all the players are in on it and keep quiet? That's a little crazy, Maura."

"He can be a little crazy," Maura said. "Like this thing with the batteries and canned food. He told me 'they' are out to get us and we have to be ready."

"'They' who?" Luis asked. "The criminals who fix the games?"

"Maybe," Maura said. "I didn't really understand."

Luis wanted to laugh but didn't. Mr. O'Hara was Maura's grandfather, and he was sick. "Well, whatever"—Luis shrugged—"this phone's useless without the pass code."

Maura had been thinking, and while she thought she frowned. Then, abruptly, her forehead cleared, and she punched in four new numbers.

Bingo. There was the home screen, and on it the beginning of a text message. *None of my business,* Luis thought, and looked away, but not before he'd read the first few words: **Hey pops so far so good.**

Maura never even pretended to look away. And then, to Luis's surprise, she swiped to read the rest of the message.

"Maura!" he protested. "It's for your grandpa. It's not okay for you—"

"I know," Maura said. "But I'm nosy."

Luis was shocked. But in the end he couldn't help it. He read the message too:

Zap, Hampton, and lights out. Thanks for your help. Delete this don't forget & CU soon. We owe you.

The sender was somebody named NB1231. Luis looked at Maura. "Do you know who that is?"

Maura didn't answer.

He elbowed her. "Maura?"

"*Ow*—what?" She looked up. "Do I know . . . ? Uh, no. But, Luis, what do you think that means? Because I don't like—"

"Scroll up," said Luis—disregarding privacy. "See if there's older messages in the string."

But there weren't. Maybe Grandpa had deleted them. This one he couldn't delete because he got sick before he saw it.

"Hey." Luis had a sudden brainstorm. "What time did that text come in anyway?"

Maura looked back at the phone. "Seven forty-two."

Luis took a breath to slow down his heart. "I don't like what I'm thinking either. Should we talk to your mom?"

"We have to," Maura said. "Come on."

On their way downstairs, Luis remembered something. "Hey, Maura—what did you use for the pass code?"

"My birthday," Maura said. "A lot of people use their own, but he's not that stuck-up."

CHAPTER FIFTEEN

rs. Brown shook her head so hard Luis thought she'd hurt her neck.

"You are being ridiculous," she told Maura. "My father would never—"

"But, Mom, just listen. It's *not* ridiculous—"

"Of course it is," Mrs. Brown said, interrupting her. "I won't have you insulting your grandfather—especially when he can't defend himself. It's some kind of dumb coincidence. How can you think anything else? Where's your loyalty to your family?"

Maura was working hard to keep her voice even. "Seven forty-two is the time the power went out. It's on Luis's clock even. Why did Grandpa say it at the hospital? Why is it the same time this message was sent? Grandpa said 'zap' just like the message too. And he bought all those survival supplies—the ones we're using now. Did he know something was going to happen?"

Mrs. Brown's face had turned pink, and a vein pulsed in her temple. When she took her father's phone, her hand was trembling. But she controlled her voice. "Dumb coincidences," she said.

"Didn't NJL do something that made Grandpa mad? Something with the money they pay retired guys every month?" Maura said.

"They cut his pension," said Mrs. Brown. "And it wasn't one bit fair. But he would never do anything wrong. He's not like that. Besides, he's old—and he's sick too. I wish people would just leave him alone, including you."

Maura looked at Luis, then at her mom. "Sorry," she said.

"Me too, Mrs. Brown," Luis said.

Maura and Luis left Mr. O'Hara's phone with Mrs. Brown and jumped on their bikes. It was eleven a.m. Joining the lukewarm chocolate milk in Luis's backpack were two heavy-duty flashlights, spare batteries, and a lantern—all borrowed from the hall closet. At the last minute, Luis had thrown in a box of granola bars too. Computer Genius would probably be hungry.

Maura and Luis tried to talk while they rode but soon

gave up. With so much traffic, navigating took all their concentration. It was a Tuesday in October, but the scene was like a summer Friday when tourists drove through on their way to the Jersey Shore. Avoiding cars was hard, and the exhaust fumes were enough to make your chest hurt.

Luis wondered who all these people were and whether his parents would soon be among them. Once they were refugees fleeing war and violence in Nicaragua. Maybe they'd be refugees all over again. Maybe they'd want him to leave with them. He couldn't play detective if he wasn't around. He would have to think of something.

In the hospital lobby, the same NJL spokesperson was on the TV. Her eyes were puffy, but her hair looked as smooth as ever. "It's true we have no timetable yet for restoration of power," she said.

The camera switched to the newsroom, and the anchorwoman announced that casualties were mounting. A whole family had suffered carbon monoxide poisoning because their home generator wasn't venting properly. A woman had fallen asleep with candles burning. She was badly burned when her house caught fire. Meanwhile, an overloaded backup generator had damaged equipment at the sewage treatment plant, and public health officials were warning people in some neighborhoods not to drink or bathe in water from the tap.

"Authorities are organizing bottled water drops at the present time, but residents should be patient," the anchorwoman said. "Now let's go to Hampton Emergency Manager Emma Perris on the line with us from city hall. Are you there, Ms. Perris?"

"I'm here, but I've only got a second."

"We know you're busy, and thanks for taking the time. Can you just tell us how your people are doing this afternoon?" the anchorwoman asked.

"Well, to be honest, we really did not need that water plant failure. It looks like the repercussions of the power outage are beginning to snowball. This thing could soon be so big we can't ride it out."

"That sounds ominous. What do you mean exactly, Ms. Perris?"

"I mean we don't have the resources on our own to cope. Mayor Manuel has already asked the governor to declare a state of emergency, which we hope will help. Our people are exhausted, and add water delivery on top of everything else . . . ? Let's just say the logistics pose a challenge. Look, thanks for your interest, but I—"

"Thank *you,* Ms. Perris. We'll let you get back to work."

Luis looked at Maura. "Did you say something about water before?" he asked.

Still staring at the TV, she nodded. "I did. And now I keep thinking this is like a movie—everything happening according to a script. Only we don't know the ending."

"The *ending*?" Luis repeated. "Talk about ominous, Maura."

Maura tore her eyes away from the screen and looked at him. "Now you're the one getting dramatic."

Luis started to argue and then remembered the confrontation with Tony at the bodega. It would have been uncool to tell Maura what happened. But he guessed it had been dramatic too—a showdown, and the good guy had won.

Maybe today he'd be the good guy again. If Mr. O'Hara was well enough to answer questions, maybe he—Luis—could do something to turn on the lights.

Or maybe he had read too many Greek myths.

"What are you smiling about?" Maura asked.

"Nothing," Luis said. "Sheesh—look at that."

The TV showed a crowd shouting, "Power to the

people!" outside the NJL offices. Police in helmets and vests faced them from behind orange barricades. When a man in a suit came out to speak to them, someone threw a rock, and he hurried back inside.

Watching the faces in the crowd turn ugly, Luis felt his stomach lurch. That building was only a few blocks away. He had walked by it a bunch of times.

"Come on." Maura grabbed his hand. "The stairway's not getting shorter while we wait."

At the fifth-floor nurse's station, Maura asked about her grandfather and learned that his condition was stable and he had been transferred to his own room.

"Are kids allowed?" Luis asked.

"Not without a guardian," the nurse said. "Do you have a guardian?"

"Yes," said Maura.

The nurse did not look up. "Sixth floor," she said.

"You are gonna get us in trouble," Luis told Maura as they climbed the last flight of stairs.

"I told the honest truth," Maura said. "I do have a guardian. She just doesn't happen to be here now."

Mr. O'Hara's new room smelled like disinfectant and old flowers. It was a shared room, and the other patient was in his own bed on the other side of a white divider curtain. He had visitors too. When Luis and Maura walked in, a middle-aged woman sitting in a chair leaned back to see who it was, then smiled weakly and raised her hand.

Luis and Maura smiled back and nodded.

Mr. O'Hara himself lay flat in bed, frail and insignificant. If anything, there were more tubes and wires than there had been the day before. Somehow, his feet had become uncovered, gnarly feet with yellow toenails and blue veins. Luis was sure Mr. O'Hara would not have wanted them exposed that way. It was undignified. Maura must have felt the same because she tugged the sheet to cover them up.

Maura and Luis approached the head of the bed. Mr. O'Hara's eyes were half open, so that he seemed to be staring at the dull green ceiling. Or maybe he had his own private TV replaying his personal greatest hits? Luis hoped that was it.

"Grandpa?" Maura leaned over and spoke quietly into his ear. "It's Maura and Luis. How do you feel?"

To Luis's surprise, Mr. O'Hara tilted his head toward Maura, blinked and grunted. Maura must not have expected this either because she started and looked up. Luis nodded encouragement. He knew what she was feeling, like they were watching someone waking from the dead.

"What, Grandpa? Are you trying to say something?"

"Show them," he mumbled. "Zap."

"He said it again. You heard it, right?" Luis said.

Maura nodded. "I heard it."

Luis leaned down and spoke into Mr. O'Hara's ear. "Do you know who caused the blackout, Mr. O'Hara? Do you know how they can fix it?"

"Luis!" Maura scolded him. "Leave him alone! You'll make him sicker."

"You heard the news, Maura," Luis said. "If your grandpa knows something—"

"My grandpa is sick," Maura said.

Luis thought of Mrs. Brown—what she'd said about family loyalty. Then he took a long breath and let it out. "Okay, I'm sorry."

"Sorry for what?" The voice came from the doorway behind Luis and Maura. "Am I interrupting? Maura, nice to see you—sorry the circumstances aren't happier."

"Uncle Nate!" said Maura.

Luis turned and saw a middle-aged white guy with a long face and short dark hair. He was wearing a suit and a purple bow tie. He smiled broadly when he saw Maura. He had small, even teeth.

"Heard this guy was laid up and thought I'd better check in on him. Hey, buddy." The man rested his hands on the bed railing and leaned over Mr. O'Hara. "Not looking too chipper. How ya feelin'?"

Mr. O'Hara did not respond.

The man stood up and spoke softly to Maura. "A stroke, was it? Jeez, that's tough."

Maura introduced the man to Luis. "This is my uncle Nate. Only he's not really my uncle."

"I used to work with Pops here and with Emily—Maura's mom," the guy said. "Families have always been friends. That sort of thing."

"Cool," said Luis. "I have lots of aunts and uncles too."

"So does he have everything he needs?" Uncle Nate asked Maura. "Rotten timing him getting sick now. When exactly was he admitted?"

Maura explained.

"I guess he hasn't woken up to say anything?" Uncle Nate asked.

"Not really," Maura said.

"So how can I help out?" Uncle Nate asked. "How are

you keeping in touch with your mom, Maura? Has she got a landline, or are you running on dead phones like everybody else?"

"No landline, but my grandpa's phone is still charged," Maura said. "My mom has it. We're going to call her in a few with the update."

Maura's uncle Nate straightened his bow tie. "So your mom's got his phone, huh. Hey, I know. Do you think she might need a ride over here later?"

Maura smiled. "That would be great, Uncle Nate. Her car is almost out of gas."

Uncle Nate looked at his watch. "I've got some TV stuff now, but as soon as I can." He turned back to the bed and leaned down. "You take care now, Mr. O'Hara. Let the médicos sort you out."

Mr. O'Hara didn't react.

Luis turned to Maura when her uncle Nate was gone. "That's the guy who works for the lady with the truck? He looks kind of familiar."

Maura nodded. "He's on TV a lot. He and my mom and my grandpa all used to work for NJL. Come on. Let's call my mom. She must be really worried by now."

There was no phone in Mr. O'Hara's room, but the

nurse at the sixth-floor nurse's station said it would be okay if Maura used the hospital's. Mrs. Brown must have had Grandpa's phone in her hand because she answered right away.

"Oh, I'm so relieved he's out of the ICU, but how does he seem?" she asked Maura after receiving the update. Her voice was loud enough that Luis could hear her too.

"He kind of seemed to know we were there," Maura said. "And one other thing, Mom." She explained about Uncle Nate.

"That's awfully kind of him," Mrs. Brown said. "So are you on your way back here now?"

"Not exactly," Maura said. "Luis and I have to get some stuff at school, maybe see his friend Carlos too. I'll be home soon."

"Wait, what?" Luis shook his head. "What are you talking about?"

Maura smiled her most innocent smile. "See you later, Mom," she said, and hung up.

hat do you mean you're coming with us to check on Computer Genius?" Luis began. He and Maura were on the stairs again, somewhere between floors three and two.

"I figured you forgot to ask me, so I saved you the trouble," Maura said. "What's the big deal?"

"The big deal is you're not coming. The big deal is it's too dangerous," Luis said.

"For a girl, you mean?" Maura said.

"For *you*," Luis said. He knew some girls went exploring, but Maura wasn't one of them.

"If it's dangerous, then you shouldn't do it either," Maura said. "But you're going to and I'm going with you. It's not like Carlos is exactly Superman. I'm pretty sure I'm stronger than him, and I'm definitely faster."

"So what? You think we're going to be running away from something?" Luis said. "Anyway, Carlos will never let you come with us."

"I didn't know Carlos was in charge," Maura said as they left the dim stairwell for the bright lobby, where the usual knot of people lingered by the TV.

The cast of characters on-screen had changed. Now a black man with gray hair was sitting at the anchor desk. "Candidate Julia Girardo has called a rally outside city hall," he said. "Mayor Manuel and Hampton police tried to discourage the assembly, but the candidate told Fox News that her supporters had the right to assemble and make known their dissatisfaction."

The picture switched to an interview with Mayor Manuel. He was a small and energetic-looking Latino with gray buzz-cut hair. In contrast to Mrs. Girardo, he spoke softly.

"It's not my intention to discourage free speech," he said, "but as a practical matter, law enforcement and indeed all the municipal authorities are overstretched and overtaxed in the ongoing emergency. We just don't have the bandwidth to handle anything more. I wish Mrs. Girardo and her supporters would respect that. It's in everyone's best interest to stay off the streets and stay safe. That's not to say we don't understand the public's frustration, and we're cooperating one hundred percent with New Jersey Light, doing our part to bring back power to the affected area."

The next face was Mrs. Girardo's: "Of course I hope my supporters will protest peacefully and obey police," she said. "At the same time, the police and the current mayor need to recognize the very real frustrations of the people on day two of this historic blackout. If the people's response is heated, if it is passionate, who can blame them?"

After that it was time for the forecast: "Temperatures are expected to dip down into the twenties tonight, bad news for residents of the blacked-out area," the woman said. "For the elderly and young children, cold temperatures can be deadly. The Red Cross will have shelters with hot food and heat available. . . ."

Luis shook his head. A rally for angry people and freezing-cold temperatures? This thing was getting worse and worse. The thought made him want to keep his friends close.

Also, Carlos most definitely was not in charge.

"Okay, you can come if you want," he told Maura.

Maura did not seem surprised that he had changed his mind. "Good. First, though, we're going to go see Beth."

"Wait, what?" said Luis. "Your sister, Beth?"

"She's the only Beth I know," Maura said.

"But where is she?" Luis asked.

"I told you," Maura said. "City hall? She's interning for the PD? Her boss is a sergeant named Anna."

"Will there be more stairs?" Luis wanted to know.

"You're worse than Carlos," Maura said.

"Why do you want to see her?" Luis asked.

"Because my grandfather knows something about what's going on," Maura said. "And we're the only ones who know that. I don't get how it fits together, but maybe the police should know."

Luis took a breath. So Maura agreed with him about this. That was a good thing. "Okay," he said, "but your mom—"

"I am not my mom," Maura said. "And I think it's important we tell somebody what Grandpa said. Maybe it will help the power company figure out what went wrong and bring the power back. If we don't tell, it's, like, our fault if the blackout goes on and on and more people get hurt."

"The police won't listen to us," Luis said.

"Sure they will. Why not?" Maura asked.

"Because we're kids, and no one listens to kids," Luis said. "No one listens to me, anyway."

"They'll listen to me," said Maura.

Outside, the sky was still clear, but there was a damp chill in the air. Luis and Maura unlocked their bicycles, rode away from the hospital entrance, and turned left onto the street. Two blocks away, city hall was a gray box with floor-to-ceiling glass on the ground floor. Four police officers stood outside, and there were half a dozen more in the lobby to stop anyone who came in and ask them about their business. Luis hung back while Maura told an officer that she and Luis were going to see her sister.

He wondered how they would've treated him if he were by himself, a Latino kid trying to get into this big building. It was strange to be with somebody who felt confident the cops were on her side.

Sure enough, the officer nodded. Then Maura turned to Luis and grinned. "No stairs this time. Officer Jenkins says the police have moved to the mayor's office on the first floor till the blackout's over. There's power there. It's this way."

The office was easy to find because light from inside streamed out the door, which had been propped open. Inside was a waiting area with chairs, every one of them occupied by a person who was either frowning or asleep. A few had magazines or papers in their laps, but no one was reading.

The police officers and staff behind the counter looked equally unhappy but more purposeful. They were bent over desks or bunched around the few working computer screens. Some were talking on the phone, voices low but intense.

Luis thought about his parents' jobs—how hard on the body they were. These people, in contrast, looked at computer screens and sat in chairs and moved paper around. It was a lot more comfortable than construction in the hot sun or cold rain, a lot more comfortable than the blood, knives, and refrigeration of packing meat— but his father could see the building when it was done, and his mother knew she had helped provide somebody's dinner.

"Do you know Beth Brown?" Maura was explaining their mission to the woman behind the counter.

"She works with Sergeant Nedza? Hold on and I'll try to find her. Family emergency?"

"Yes," said Maura.

The woman disappeared into another room. Standing beside her, Luis reached for his phone for the hundredth time, then remembered. Maura rolled her eyes.

"So how come you're so used to not having a phone

already?" Luis asked her. "How come you're such a morally superior person?"

"It's not moral superiority. It's discipline," said Maura.

"I got discipline," Luis said. "I do a hundred push-ups every morning . . . if I remember."

"How about this morning?" Maura asked him.

"This morning there's a power blackout in case you haven't noticed," said Luis. "It was not a normal morning."

"You need light to do push-ups?" Maura asked.

"I wouldn't want to bump my nose," Luis said.

The woman came back.

"She'll be right—," the woman started to say, but before she could finish, Maura's sister came through a doorway at the back of the room. Luis hadn't seen her since before she went to college. Wearing a dress and nice shoes, Beth almost looked like a grown-up herself. She was frowning, anxious.

"How's Grandpa?" Beth asked from halfway across the room, and everyone turned to look at her. "Is Mom okay?"

Maura didn't answer till Beth reached the counter. "He's out of the ICU. Mom's okay, just worried."

"Oh, good." Beth breathed again and cocked her head. "I'm so busy here, and it's not easy to check in. Hey, Luis."

"Hey, Beth."

"Can we talk to you in, uh . . . private?" Maura asked, and Luis wondered if she had heard that phrase on a TV show.

"Ha—there's not a lot of 'private' around," Beth said. "But come on back to the desk I'm using. Nobody's got time to pay attention."

Maura and Luis went around the counter, then followed Beth through two doorways, each of which led to a maze of cubicles. At last she came to her own desk, on which sat a dark computer monitor and many piles of paper. Surrounding them was a hum of voices.

Beth dropped into the chair and faced her sister. "Okay, shoot."

"Grandpa knows something about the blackout, how it started, I mean," Maura said.

Beth ducked her chin and raised her eyebrows. *Keep talking.*

Maura told her about 742 and zap and the mysterious text. "Plus, remember how he went out and bought all that emergency stuff a couple of weeks ago? Pretty coincidental, don't you think?"

"What does Mom say?" Beth asked.

"Mom doesn't want to believe it," Maura said.

"Do you?" said Beth.

"Of course not, but come on. It's too weird."

Beth took a breath. "It's weird all right, but it could still be a coincidence. Anyway, I don't know what we can do about it. He's not well enough to answer our questions or NJL's either."

"Can't the police investigate?" Maura said. "You know, look at his cell phone to see who he's been calling. Confiscate his computer . . . find out who sent that text and talk to them . . . I dunno—police stuff."

"Beth?" A compact, athletic-looking woman looked over the cubicle wall. "Oh, hi—you've got to be Beth's sister. Maura, right? I'm Anna. Good to meet you—who's your friend?"

Maura introduced Luis, and that was the end of chit-chat. "I need Beth back now, okay?" Anna said. "I guess it's obvious we're pretty busy. Come say hi when we're back to normal. We're giving Beth a trial by fire."

"It is kind of exciting," Beth said.

"Good woman," said Anna. "And besides, it could be worse. Nobody's bleeding in the street for now. Up and at 'em, Beth. Julia Girardo, in her infinite wisdom, is holding a rally in the square later this afternoon. We've gotta deploy our people now."

This was Beth's chance to tell her boss that the kids had an idea about the blackout. It might be worthless, or it might not be. Beth could do that, or she could disregard her little sister and get back to work.

"Guys, I'll see you later," Beth said. "And I'll think about what you told me, pass it on if I have a chance. Okay?"

Maura tried to argue. "But, *Beth* . . ."

Anna had already walked away. Beth was on her feet. "Gotta go," she said, and followed.

Luis and Maura didn't say a word until they were outside. The temperature had dropped some more, and clouds covered the sun. It was too early in the season to snow, wasn't it? That would be all the city needed.

"Okay." Maura put her hands on her hips and scowled. "Let me have it, Luis. You were totally right. I never should've thought anybody'd listen to kids—not even my own sister."

Luis had looked forward to saying "I told you so." Now there was no point. "Maybe it's good that we're on our own." He tried to sound optimistic even though he didn't feel it. "Hey—what's going on over there?"

A few people had gathered in the square across from city hall. Some carried signs—JULIA HAS ALL THE ANSWERS, TAKE BACK OUR CITY, WE WANT POWER!

"It must be the rally Beth's boss was talking about," Maura said.

Something about the scene made Luis think of Mrs. Brown explaining a generator. *The people waiting around are like electrons in a wire,* he thought. *They're waiting for something to get them going—turn them into current. I wonder what will happen when it does.* Then he remembered seeing the guy throw the rock on TV. Suddenly it seemed even more important to do something, but Maura was feeling defeated.

"How are we supposed to do anything?" she asked. "We don't have computers or big trucks or cranes. We don't have money. We don't even have a screwdriver."

"Yeah, we do," said Luis, "if I can find the toolbox in our basement, I mean. And we have something else, too—at least we do if we can find him. We have Computer Genius."

ifteen minutes later Maura and Luis walked into Señora Álvaro's bodega to meet Carlos. The store no longer smelled either like vomit or like humans, either. Now it smelled like vinegar. Shoppers had purchased everything, right down to the last roll of waxed paper. Humming as she worked, Señora Álvaro was spraying the bare shelves with vinegar water and wiping them down.

Carlos, meanwhile, was mopping. He was not humming, and when he saw his friends he grinned like a jailed man set free.

"Oh, jeez, I thought you'd never get here," he said. "Gotta go, Señora Álvaro. Thanks a lot for uh . . . letting me work for you." He almost dropped the mop in his haste.

"When the floor's done, I'll pay you," Señora Álvaro said. Then she looked at Luis. "Dígame, how was Computer Genius yesterday when you saw him? With everything else, I forgot even to ask. Is he okay? Did he drink the chocolate milk?"

Luis should've been ready for the question, but he wasn't. "Uh, that is, I dunno exactly. How long does chocolate milk last anyway?"

Señora Álvaro scowled. "Didn't you find him when I told you?"

"We'll go find him now," Maura said. "While Carlos finishes mopping."

"Great idea." Luis was halfway out the door.

"Take him something to eat!" Señora Álvaro told them. "That boy does not take care of himself."

In Luis's neighborhood there were something like thirty abandoned houses. Big factories had moved out of Hampton years ago. Jobs went with them, people moved, and the price of houses fell. The ones that had been abandoned were the ones worth less than fixing them up would cost. Luis could remember when people had lived in some of them. Others had been empty his whole life. By now most of the houses had so much damage inside—collapsed walls, gaping holes in the floor, caved-in roofs—that even Computer Genius snubbed them.

The ones in better shape had been claimed by gangs for buying and selling, or for meeting their girlfriends. Computer Genius was clueless about a lot of things but not about gangs. Migrating from house to house, he made deals with them and carved out territory, whatever it took to survive.

Now that he wasn't in a hurry to get to school, Luis was confident he'd find the genius. He didn't expect any help from Maura, but it was Maura who stopped and pointed. "I say that one."

Unlike most of the houses on the block, the one she'd selected still had address numbers stuck to the siding—316, which would make it 316 Larch. There was an ancient, sturdy tree in front. The top branches reached for the roof as if they wanted to give it a hug.

"What do you mean? You don't know what you're talking about," Luis said. "You've never even hunted Computer Genius before."

"There's such a thing as beginner's luck," said Maura. "See that Arby's wrapper in the puddle there? He likes Arby's, you told me. And a blanket's hung up to block that busted-window up there."

"It's too empty-looking," said Luis. "I'm not getting

the vibe. Let's see if Carlos is done mopping. He's pretty good at this."

Back at the bodega, Señora Álvaro was taping another sign to the door: CLOSED/CERRADO UNTIL THE LIGHTS COME BACK.

"¿Tuviste suerte? Any luck?" she asked.

"Not yet, but Carlos will find him, right, Carlos?" Luis said.

"Right," Carlos said. "Uh, Señora, can I have my hourly now? My pay, I mean?"

Beneath the cash register on the counter was a drawer. Señora Álvaro opened it, reached in, and pulled out a package of gummi worms. "I keep these for Luis," she said. "Today he does not deserve them."

If Carlos was disappointed to have candy instead of cash, he didn't show it. "More for me," he said. "Gracias."

Luis tried not to be annoyed—even though he was thinking it was lucky for Señora Álvaro he had stopped by the night before. Meanwhile, she was talking: "My daughter, Rosa, and I are going to stay with my sister in Gloucester. It's better than a shelter and not so cold as here."

"Does she know you're coming?" Maura asked.

"Rosa's phone is still charged, believe it or not. My

sister was very glad to hear from us. From TV, she thought in Hampton corre la sangre en las calles—blood in the streets—but I told her only broken glass. Luis, you have something of mine. Can you keep it a little longer?"

"Sure, Señora, no problem," Luis said. "Quizás you pay me in gummi worms too?"

"Quizás—perhaps," Señora Álvaro repeated. "Ahora go find the genius."

They all said adiós and buena suerte after that. The three kids were barely out the door when Carlos asked Luis what he was keeping for the señora.

Luis was tempted to tell him. Being trusted with all that money made him feel important. He wouldn't mind if other people thought he was important too. But he didn't tell. If he told Carlos, he might as well put the video up on YouTube.

"Nada," Luis said. "Nothing. Let's go find Computer Genius. Look what I brought." Luis opened his backpack and pulled out the heavy-duty flashlights.

"Let there be luz!" Carlos said. "But, uh . . . what's *she* doing here?" He nodded at Maura.

"Coming with you," Maura announced. "I've already found where the genius is staying too. Follow me."

"She's persistent," said Luis.

"It's fine with me if you come," Carlos told Maura. "Sometimes when we need to carry a stone-cold dead body out of a house, it's good to have help."

"Give it up, Carlos. You can't gross me out," Maura said.

Soon they were back at 316 Larch.

"What do you think?" Luis asked Carlos.

"Arby's, check." Carlos nodded. "And the window too. Por supuesto puedes probarlo—give it a try."

"How do we get in?" Maura asked. "Climb the tree? There's not even a knob on the door."

Luis glanced right and left down the street, then turned on his flashlight. "Watch the master."

Two steps to the stoop, and he was at the door. He put his shoulder to it, leaned forward, and shoved hard.

The door gave no resistance, and he all but tumbled inside.

"Oh." Maura nodded. "Like that."

"Exactamente," Carlos said. "You go next . . . unless by now you're afraid?"

"Not me." Maura turned on her flashlight and followed Luis. A moment later all three of them stood in what had been a living room, only now there were two old tires where chairs should have been, a pile of swollen black garbage bags in the corner, and an upside-down sofa spilling its stuffing.

"Be careful where you step," Luis said. Maura aimed her light at the floor and saw broken bottles, pulled-up floorboards, and oozing speckled spots of dampness. With the windows boarded up, the air felt thick and smelled like rotting vegetables and something else—animals?

"What's that smell?" She wrinkled her nose.

"The blood of those that came before," said Carlos in his best Transylvanian accent.

"All the houses smell like this," Luis said. "It's garbage mostly, and the rats probably have a lot to do with it. Did I mention the rats before?"

"You left out the rats." Maura shuddered. "But I'm here now, and I'm staying. So what do we do? Do we yell?" Up to this point they had been talking quietly, respectful of the ghosts . . . or maybe the rats.

Luis was no longer creeped out by abandoned houses. He almost liked the smell because he associated it with adventure—like the smell of the jungle to a jungle explorer, he guessed. Odysseus had "the wine-dark sea" with the Cyclops, Scylla and Charybdis, and the sirens. Luis had the abandoned houses with their crumbling walls and ghostly echoes—a place to prove his courage and his cunning.

It was his brother, Reynaldo, who had first sneaked him into one. Luis must have been about four. Reynaldo told him later his idea had been to scare Luis away from the houses forever. It was a plan that did not work.

Luis was nine the first time he ran into Computer Genius. Before that he had only heard the legend. That day the genius was fast asleep in a pile of blankets. When Luis's footsteps woke him up, he sat up, and Luis almost had a heart attack. *It's alive!*

Seeing the kid so shaken, Computer Genius had offered him a can of beer. Luis took it and discovered he didn't like the taste or the headache he got later.

"There are no rules in abandoned houses," Luis told Maura now. "¿Hola?" he yelled. "Yo—Genius, you here?"

They waited for a count of five but no answer.

"Like I said, wrong house," Luis said.

Carlos gave it a try. "Olly-olly hola, Genius!" he called. "You upstairs or what?"

Another count of five. Luis was about to say, "Vamos,

let's go," when they all heard a *thump*. Someone taking a step? Something falling? It could be the genius or a raccoon or the tree branches moving outside.

Maura said, "Things that go bump in the night." She was trying to be funny, but her voice quavered.

"It's the middle of the afternoon, Maura. Don't go all *girl* on us," said Luis.

"Yeah," said Carlos. "Girls—*jeez*."

"Let's go upstairs and look," Luis said.

As they moved, the beams of the flashlights made a slideshow out of the sad, decaying house—a patch of faded wallpaper, the splintered newel post, holes in the floorboards, a pile of ragged, stinking drapes. It took forever to climb the stairs. Twice Luis felt the wood crack under his weight.

Upstairs, there was enough light from outside that they could turn off their flashlights. The breeze blew in through the busted windows, and the fresh air smelled good.

"Computer Genius?" Luis spoke in a normal voice.

"Who's that?" came back the answer.

Is that him? Maura mouthed.

"No. It's a talking raccoon," said Carlos.

"Are you okay, Genius? Where are you?" Luis asked.

"I'm hungry," said the voice, "and I . . . I don't feel so good. What's going on? Can you guys help me out?"

They found Computer Genius in what had been the front bedroom. He was huddled in blankets on a mattress in a corner. Two planks of plywood had fallen from the windows so the light of the gloomy day shone in.

Computer Genius remained flat on his back. "Did you bring a phone charger? Did you bring food?"

Social graces were not Computer Genius's thing.

Luis handed over a bottle of water and the box of granola bars. He wished he had brought baby wipes or something the genius could use to clean his hands and face. Even in the bad light, he looked pale, his skin gray-white like a mushroom. Flecks of stubble dotted his chin and jaw. His hair was black and unkempt, not long but uneven, as if it had been cut with dull scissors or a knife.

Maybe it was a blessing that they couldn't see him or his bedding too clearly. Maybe it was a blessing that in the thicket of smells, the smell of the genius and his blankets did not stand out.

"Have you been stuck up here all by yourself since yesterday?" Maura's voice was full of sympathy.

"Who are you?" Computer Genius replied. "What did you bring me?"

Before Maura could answer, Carlos spoke. "You don't look so good, Genius," he said. "And for you, that's saying something."

"When I've got nothing to do, I hibernate," the genius said. "Right now there's nothing to do. I could use some Advil, though."

"I've got chocolate milk," Luis said.

Maura made a face. "It's gotta be sour by now."

"That stuff from the bodega?" The genius propped himself up on his elbows, tore the wrapping from a granola bar with his teeth, and took a bite. "It never goes bad."

Luis unzipped his backpack and handed the carton over. Computer Genius opened it immediately and swallowed a gulp. Luis, Maura, and Carlos watched, fascinated. What did spoiled chocolate milk do to a person anyway?

Nothing terrible, apparently.

Computer Genius wiped his mouth with the back of his hand. "I could still use Advil."

Maura started to explain about the blackout, but Computer Genius raised a hand to silence her. "That means nothing to me," he said. "I need something. Logistics of obtaining it—they are up to you."

"Genius," Luis broke in. "We'll get you the Advil. But there's a problem, and maybe you can help."

"Everyone's got a problem," Computer Genius said.

"Ours is the blackout," Luis said.

"Wait . . . what?" Carlos said. "I thought we were just here—"

"To make sure the genius is okay," said Luis. "But at the same time, maybe he can help us."

The genius sat up, straightened his blankets, and unwrapped another granola bar. Meanwhile, Luis explained about the blackout, how there were rumors it might be a cyberattack.

"So you want me to take a look at the power company's system and see what I can find." Computer Genius was fully awake by now.

How old is he anyway? Luis wondered. *Or maybe I don't want to know. If he has a human age, it makes him less of a legend.*

"No problem," Computer Genius said at last. "But I need a few things."

"Dígame," Luis said.

"A twelve-pack of Red Bull. Five—no, make it six— cans of Cheddar Cheese Pringles. A charged battery for my phone, or a charger. There's no Wi-Fi with the power out. I'll have to use the phone as a hot spot."

Luis had no idea how they were going to charge the genius's phone or get any of the other stuff for that matter. But he tried to sound confident. "Give us your phone, then."

Computer Genius was surprisingly quick to locate it among the mess of blankets.

"Okay." Luis took the phone and stuffed it into his backpack. "We'll be back before dark."

"Where I live, it's always dark," the genius said. "And one more thing."

"Skittles?" said Carlos. "Hershey's Kisses? Chips Ahoy!?"

"Cash dollars," said Computer Genius. "Call it two hundred for now, but I reserve the right to up my fees. The job could turn out to be harder than I think."

Luis had not anticipated this. "Uh . . . , no offense, but what's a guy like you need money for?"

"I'm saving for a wall-to-wall carpet," the genius said.

"You're kidding, right?" Carlos said.

The genius did not crack a smile.

"Okay, I'll get you money," said Luis.

Carlos looked at him. "How—"

Luis didn't know how, but he knew he would think of something. That's what heroes did, right? He would be resourceful like his hero Odysseus. "Never mind. I'll get it," he said. "Genius, do you want us to leave you a flashlight?"

"No need." Computer Genius lay back and pulled up the covers. "Till you come back, I'm gonna kick back, zone out, and get me some beauty rest."

Luis was the first one out.

Carlos followed him, blinking. "My man?" he said as he tripped down the steps.

"Yo?" Luis said. It was always strange to emerge from the twilight world of an abandoned house into daylight— like rejoining the living.

"Is there something you forgot to tell me, hue?" Carlos asked. "What the heck?"

Luis shrugged. "Maybe he can help. Anyway, it won't hurt."

"You are welcome for how I played it cool," said Carlos.

"And where are we going to get that kind of money?"

"Not your problem," Luis said.

Maura, meanwhile, was shaking her head. "That's the guy that's gonna help us? He looks like *he* belongs in the hospital."

"He's okay," Carlos said.

"He'll be fine," Luis said.

"Not if he's living on Red Bull and Pringles," Maura said. "I am going to bring him some apples. Who doesn't like apples?"

"Suit yourself," Luis said. "Pero lo más importante, can you charge the phone?"

Maura nodded. "At the hospital. But what about the other stuff?"

"My mom's got Advil," Carlos said. "But I don't know about Pringles or Red Bull."

"I'll think of something," Luis said. He was on his bike by now, coasting in tight circles. "Meet back here at five. And don't tell anybody what we're doing. We don't want to get the genius in trouble. We're just trying to find out what's what. You know?"

"*Oooh*—top secret!" Carlos said. "I like it."

CHAPTER EIGHTEEN

Luis took off in a hurry, his thoughts moving as fast as his pedals. Two blocks from home, he overtook a posse of teens riding low-slung bikes. They were doing tricks and getting in the way of the few cars on the road.

"*Hey—hey—hey!*" they hollered at Luis, and a couple tried to cut him off. Luis had to make a right and go down an alley to get away. When he stopped to listen and take a breath, his heart was racing like his thoughts.

Had Tony been with those kids?

That guy took a lot of stupid risks, but he was smart in some ways, knew how to keep his guys loyal. In a scary world, he told them he had their backs.

I got lucky last night, Luis thought. *If they hadn't been drinking, things might've turned out different.*

Right now Luis knew one thing for sure. He did not want to see those guys on bikes again. To avoid them, he cut through vacant lots and rode down alleys—made the two-block trip to his house twice as long.

Indoors at last, he called, "¿Hola?" but there was no answer.

The front room was freezing—colder than the air outside. Luis's fingers were numb from gripping the handlebars of his bike, and he flexed his hands to warm them up. Then he rolled the bike into his room, leaned it against the wall, and stuck his toe under the bed to check for the box. Still there. When he bent down to look, the money was still there too.

Once in a movie on TV he had heard it called lettuce. Stale lettuce, he thought now, because it was limp and grimy. It had its own peculiar smell.

Only then did the idea come into his head: The señora's money might be the solution to his problem. Spend a little on the genius. Bring back the power. What did you call that? An investment? The señora knew all about business. She would understand that, right?

A voice in Luis's head argued. It was wrong to take her money. Señora Álvaro had trusted him. He was violating her trust.

He fought with himself but only for a moment. People were getting hurt because the power was out. If the blackout continued, people might die. This was important.

With no idea how much he might need, Luis counted out two hundred and fifty dollars in fives and twenties. He tried not to think too hard about how he was going to repay it or how mad Señora Álvaro was going to be.

Counting done, Luis grabbed a spiral notebook from his desk, tore out paper, and wrote "IOU $250, Luis Cardenal." Then he put the paper in the box and closed it.

Luis was retrieving a sweater from his dresser when he heard his brother's voice. "¿Hola? ¿Luis? ¿Estás aquí? Are you here?"

"Sí, aquí—in my room."

Reynaldo appeared in his doorway, frowning. Reynaldo was big and broad enough to have played football. What he didn't have was killer instinct. Papá said he didn't have a mean bone in his body, and Papá didn't mean it as a compliment, either. Like Luis, Reynaldo had an angular face with a strong jawline. He worked in an auto shop and liked to dress well on his days off. That day he was wearing jeans and a long-sleeved blue polo under a trim down jacket.

"So how do you like this garbage?" Reynaldo spread his arms, and Luis knew he meant the blacked-out area. "They're saying the power won't ever come back. The company can't make money on poor people, so they're going to abandon us, let the lines fall down and ignite the city, burn it up."

Luis shook his head. "That's not right."

"What do you mean not right? Nobody cares about us. We're all a bunch of bad hombres. They'll bulldoze our houses and plant Jersey tomatoes for rich people to eat, or give the whole place back to the bears in the forest."

"Es posible," Luis said. "But till they do, do you got gas in your car?"

"Do I have gas? Soy tu hermano, Luis, but I guess you don't know me at all. Of course, I have gas."

"Bueno," Luis said. "Because I've got some stuff I've got to buy. Maybe you can take me somewhere normal, somewhere with electricity?"

"Is it important?" Reynaldo said.

"Yeah, it's important," Luis said.

"Because there's only so much gas around, and I don't want to waste it," Reynaldo said.

"You sound like Mrs. Brown—Maura's mother," Luis

said. "She shared food with me, but she wouldn't offer any to the neighbors. It was weird, like all of a sudden she got greedy."

"Are you calling your own brother 'greedy'?" Reynaldo said.

"What do you call it?" Luis asked.

"I call it careful," Reynaldo said. "We don't know what's gonna happen—we gotta look out for ourselves first. Anyway, my car's at my house. With work shut down, I have no place to be in a hurry, so I'm traveling on foot. You up for a hike?"

Luis shook his head. "No good. No time. What I need is Red Bull and Cheddar Cheese Pringles. Any ideas?"

Reynaldo raised his eyebrows and crossed his arms. "Red Bull and Cheddar Cheese Pringles is an emergency?" Luis didn't answer, and Reynaldo shrugged. "There's a kind of like flea market over by the stadium. Looks like people have brought in necessities from out of town."

"From out of town, or stolen?" Luis asked. "Stores got broken into last night."

"Either way I bet it's pricey. I can come with you if you want," Reynaldo said.

"I wouldn't mind company," Luis said.

Reynaldo was eighteen years older than his little brother; their father sometimes called him the third parent. If Papá thought this was a joke, Luis did not. It was Reynaldo who reminded Luis to wear a bike helmet, eat breakfast, and stay out of fights. It was Reynaldo who demanded to see his report cards.

Reynaldo had had the same job at the garage since he graduated from high school. He didn't drink much. He was saving his money because he wanted a house and a family . . . someday. Even though Reynaldo would be thirty on his next birthday, it wasn't clear when someday might arrive.

It was a half-mile walk to the ballpark. On the way, Reynaldo wanted to know for real what was the so-called emergency.

"I got a friend that lives in one of the houses," Luis said. "I guess he's hungry."

"You mean Computer Genius?" Reynaldo said.

"Quizás—maybe," Luis said.

"Hey, you remember that time when you were a kid and you started the fire in one of the houses?" Reynaldo asked.

Luis nodded. "You told me you'd kill me if you caught me with matches again."

"I would've too," Reynaldo said.

"You know that doesn't make any sense, right?" Luis said. "You didn't want me with matches because I might hurt myself. So you were going to hurt me for having matches?"

Reynaldo shrugged. "It made perfect sense," he said. "It gave you two reasons not to fool around with matches. Hey—I heard another rumor about the blackout. The whole thing's part of an attack by a foreign power, like the Japanese attack on Pearl Harbor during World War II."

"What foreign power? I thought Japan was on our side now," Luis said.

"There's countries that aren't on our side," Reynaldo said. "And international terrorists too. Don't you go to the movies? Don't you watch the news?"

Luis remembered the gossip at Señora Álvaro's bodega. "But why attack Hampton?" Luis wanted to know. "Like you said, nobody cares about a bunch of poor brown people. If they wanted to get attention, they'd go after Beverly Hills or Manhattan."

Reynaldo pondered for a minute, then shrugged. "Maybe they're not that smart. Anyway, if it is a war, then our military will have to fight back some way. Maybe the army will knock out electricity in the other country or skip that and go straight to nuclear weapons."

All this made Luis think about what Maura had said— how real life was playing out like a movie script, only no one knew the ending. And if nuclear bombs were involved, then maybe "ending" was the right word.

Did Mr. O'Hara really have something to do with it? What about Mrs. Brown and her job at NJL? Someone had sent Mr. O'Hara that text message, but who?

The chance that the leader of another country was behind it all seemed too crazy. But then the whole thing was crazy, wasn't it?

"Here we are." Reynaldo interrupted Luis's thoughts. "Take a look over there." The ballpark parking lot, largest field of asphalt in Hampton, had become a spontaneous marketplace. Scattered here and there were two dozen cars, each with its trunk popped, and an equal number of vans. Massed around each vehicle was a knot of shoppers. Some of them seemed to be waving cash.

Luis turned his head to take it in. "How did this happen? How did people even find out about it?"

Reynaldo grinned. "It's like toadstools," he said. "The growing conditions were right, and there you go. As for how they found out—same way I did. A guy tells another one, or somebody sees it when they pass by."

Luis's brain fast-forwarded. The blackout keeps on, more cars and more shoppers, people pitching tents, paying security guys, digging gardens, electing a mayor . . . After a while they'd set up their own power grid—a new city on the ruins of the old one, like a video game only for real.

"I was just thinking the world was going to end," Luis said. "But this is more like some kind of weird beginning."

"If you say so, bro," Reynaldo said. "Me? I'm just hoping the power comes back before everything blows up."

The sellers had organized themselves according to what they were offering—food, water, coats and blankets, flashlights, cans of gasoline, hardware, battery-powered radios and TVs, cell phones, chargers, batteries, pills, alcohol, and cigarettes. A couple of people had generators for sale, but they weren't attracting much interest. Too expensive, probably.

"It's like Walmart only outdoors," said Reynaldo.

"More shouting than at Walmart," said Luis.

It was obvious a lot of cash was changing hands. How long before some bad actor figured out how much cash was here for the taking? Were these pop-up shopkeepers ready for that?

"Bingo." Reynaldo pointed. "This gentleman's got you."

Half a dozen people were buying from the pudgy black guy in an old colorless Audi. He was stocking snack food, cereal, and soda. "How much for a four-pack of Red Bull and Cheddar Cheese Pringles?" Luis asked. Then he thought of something else, "Oh, and do you have baby wipes?"

Luis half expected him to say "aisle six," only he didn't. "I don't do toiletries," he said. "The Red Bull's twenty. Plain Pringles only, and they're five."

Luis didn't answer right away. So much money!

"You don't want it, someone else does," the guy said.

Luis handed over two bills from Señora Álvaro's stash. "How about a bag?" Luis asked the seller.

"Do I look like I have a bag?" he said.

Luis zipped Genius's goods into his backpack.

"Where'd you get the dollars?" Reynaldo asked.

"Here and there," Luis said, "you know, helping out."

"And you're spending it on the genius?" Reynaldo asked.

Luis shrugged. "It's more of a trade. Anyway, I still

need wipes and maybe deodorant." He wished he had thought to ask Carlos for those things.

Reynaldo rolled his eyes. "Somebody didn't raise you right. We got the apocalypse going on, and you want to be sure you smell nice."

The woman most likely to have wipes also had soap, shampoo, and paper towels. Only one roll of toilet paper remained in the trunk of her twenty-year-old blue Caddy. Two women were arguing over who had spotted it first, a nice predicament for the seller, who could probably have asked any amount of money.

Luis was glad he wanted wipes, only ten dollars—"a *steal* and they're top quality, too, a name brand," the woman pointed out.

"Do you have any deodorant?" Luis asked.

"Hang on a sec." The woman walked around to the passenger side of the car, opened the door, closed it, and came over with a stick of Ban.

"Great," said Luis. "How much?"

"Five," said the woman.

Luis gave her the cash, then had second thoughts and removed the lid. "Hey!" he protested. "This is used!"

The woman shrugged. "Sure, hon, but I'm clean."

Luis said, "¡Guácala! Gross!" and tried to hand it back, but she wouldn't take it. "Like the sign says, all sales final."

"The sign does not say that," Luis pointed out.

"It will in a minute. Besides, the deodorant still works. See if it doesn't."

Reynaldo couldn't stop laughing.

By this time the sun was dropping below the outline of the skyscrapers across the river. Luis checked his watch— quarter to five. He told his perplexed brother adiós, gracias, gotta be somewhere, then jogged home to get his bike. With luck, he would be only a couple of minutes late.

CHAPTER NINETEEN

Maura was already outside the house at 316 Larch when Luis arrived. Waiting for Carlos, they caught each other up. When Maura saw Mr. O'Hara at the hospital, he was pretty much the same as before, but one of his roommate's visitors had told her that earlier he'd been restless and mumbling.

"Maybe that's good. Maybe he's getting stronger," Luis said.

"I hope," Maura said.

"Did you see your mom?" Luis asked.

"The nurse said she hadn't been there," Maura said. "I guess Uncle Nate hasn't been able to pick her up yet."

"So what about charging the phone?" Luis asked.

"A lot of people had the same idea as us," Maura said. "The security guys were chasing people out and yanking chargers from the wall. It turns out only certain outlets work—they're called red outlets. They're the ones on circuits hooked up to the generators."

Luis got a bad feeling. "Does that mean you didn't do it?"

"Give me some credit," Maura said. "I was freezing my tush outside the hospital when I thought of Beth's office. Not so many people go in and out of there. So I went back. Beth wasn't at her desk, but I found an outlet near it on the floor and plugged in. Beth came back a little later."

"Did you tell her what you were doing?" Luis asked.

"I said since she wouldn't help us, we were helping ourselves. I think she felt a little guilty, so she said go ahead, provided nobody else tried to throw me out. And nobody did."

"Hiciste bien—you did good," Luis said.

"Gracias," Maura said. "Do you think Carlos is coming? It's almost five thirty."

Luis shrugged. "He's not always that reliable. Maybe we should go in without him."

Half an hour later, Maura and Luis were sitting on either side of Computer Genius in the private second-floor rat's nest. He had been disappointed by the lack of Advil and the Pringles being plain, and Luis had had to promise an upgrade as soon as possible.

Now outfitted with seriously large headphones, Computer Genius bobbed his chin and drummed his fingers on the keyboard of his laptop. Luis could hear the music too. Before all of them on the screen scrolled line after line of glowing white computer code. It was meaningless to Luis—letters separated by slashes, spaces, and unintelligible punctuation.

Maura seemed to understand a little. "It's computer language," she explained. "The genius found a way through the firewall of the NJL system, and he pulled up the code that runs the grid. That's what he's looking at. He's trying to find the malware."

"The what?" Luis said.

"Malware. In other words, the commands—the lines of code—that were inserted by an intruder to mess things up."

"You mean to turn off the lights?" Luis was trying hard to understand.

"It's probably more complicated than that. Maybe more like to do something that did something that caused something else—and then that turned off the lights," Maura said.

Scowling at the screen, Luis shook his head "But there's so much of it! Isn't it like looking for a misspelled word in the encyclopedia?"

"More like an out-of-place sentence, a statement,"

Maura said. "But if you know about this stuff, you can use an analyzer to find anything suspicious. You know how you can search in a document? It's like that."

"What are you looking for exactly?" Luis asked.

Maura shook her head. "It's not like I'm an expert," she said. "But the way I understand it, there are certain patterns of code that malware uses a lot. So you tell the analyzer to look for those patterns."

Luis thought for a moment. "But what if it's brand-new malware? What if it uses different patterns?" Luis hoped he sounded like he knew what he was talking about.

"If it's new, it could be a problem," Maura agreed. "It kind of depends on how clever the hacker is. Like anything else, there are smart ones and not so smart ones. We have to hope we're up against one that isn't so smart."

But in that case, Luis thought as he watched the bright lines of code scroll by, *wouldn't the power company's IT people have figured the problem out by now?*

Suddenly, with obvious effort, Computer Genius yanked the headphones off his head, tore his eyes away from the screen, and shook himself the way a wet dog does.

"What's up?" Luis said. "Did you fix it? Are the lights back on?"

"If they are, I didn't do it," Computer Genius said. "But I think I see what's going on. Looks like they used a RAT to drop a logic bomb into the SCADA. Luckily there's a mistake in the suicide script. You know what that is, right?"

"Sure." Luis nodded. "Rodent go boom. Got it."

Maura grinned, but not Computer Genius. "What do they teach you kids in school these days?" he asked.

"Hey—you're pretty much a kid too, you know," Luis said.

"I inhabit a different frame of reference," Genius said.

"Unh-hunh," Luis said.

"A suicide script is a Windows batch file, right?" Computer Genius spoke with exaggerated slowness. "It's supposed to delete the executable file—in this case the logic bomb—as soon as it's done its job. Then it's supposed to destroy itself so somebody like me can't find it."

Luis nodded. "I see," he said. "The suicide script is supposed to erase the file that did the job, then erase itself. And what's the rest of what you said? I guess a rat isn't a rodent?"

"It's a remote-access Trojan," Computer Genius said.

"You mean like the Trojan horse?" Luis said.

The genius looked blank.

"Troy? Greeks? *The Odyssey*?" Luis said.

"Enlighten me." Computer Genius leaned back against the pillows.

Luis said sure, happy that for once he knew something. "So, like, a long, long time ago some Greek dudes gave some Trojan dudes a giant wooden horse as a present," he began. "Giant meaning like an apartment building, and it was on wheels for easy transportation. The Trojans and the Greeks had been fighting, so you'd think the Trojans would've been suspicious, but I guess they were pretty excited about such a big present, and they rolled it inside the walls of their city and partied hard and passed out."

"I have a bad feeling about this," said Maura.

"Bad for the Trojans," Luis said. "As soon as they were out of the way, the Greek soldiers hiding inside the horse opened it up, climbed out, and massacred everybody."

Computer Genius nodded. "Yeah, I see. It is the same deal," he said. "But instead of a horse, it's a software module, and instead of soldiers, it's files that are designed to attack."

"What's the 'R'—the remote part?" Luis asked.

"The system was accessed remotely," said Genius,

"same way I'm doing it now. The original hacker might've used an e-mail to somebody inside the system, like somebody who works for NJL. When that guy opened an attachment, an exploit found a vulnerability in the browser software and dropped its payload."

Exploit? Vulnerability? Payload? Luis didn't understand every word, but he got the gist. "And according to you, there was a mistake," Luis said.

"Call it a typo," Computer Genius said. "The suicide script was supposed to delete a file named 'wiper.sh.' But the attackers told it to delete a file called 'viper.sh'—with a 'v,' not a 'w,' get it?"

"Maybe they ran out of Red Bull," Maura said.

Again, the genius did not smile. "It happens. And because of the mistake, the script couldn't find itself to delete itself, and a bunch of evidence got left behind."

Luis nodded. It wasn't quite as complicated as he had expected. "Okay, so there's one thing I don't get. How come if you know so much the lights aren't back on?"

"Even though I can see the malware, I don't know what it told the system to do," Computer Genius said. "To figure that out, I'd need to know more about the SCADA, the PLCs and all the equipment at New Jersey Light. There are probably hundreds, maybe thousands, of different devices in the system. Somehow or another, the bad guys told some of them, or one of them, to shut down . . . , but what device and how was it affected? I have no idea."

"And you think the New Jersey Light IT people don't know either?" Maura asked.

"It doesn't look like it," the genius said. "Otherwise the lights would be back. What you have to get is how complicated the system is. Even for experts, it could take a long time to sort it out. You have to look at every piece of equipment to do it."

Luis felt crushed. Computer Genius was so smart. He knew so much. He had explained so much. Luis had been sure the blackout was about to be over. Now, all of a sudden—forget about it.

Then Luis had another thought—one he didn't like. "Genius," he said, "how do we know *you* didn't hack the grid and turn off the lights?"

"*Luis!*" Maura said, but the genius only shrugged.

"You don't know for sure," he admitted. "But if it was me, I'd already've turned the lights back on. Then I could collect my pay and watch Star Trek reruns. No more hard work and having to think so much."

Speaking of having to think . . . Luis's head was spin-ning. If the genius was the hacker, then he, Luis, might as well give up. He didn't want to give up. Therefore, whether it was true or not, he had to decide that the genius wasn't the hacker.

Maura seemed to be way ahead of Luis. "Are you say-ing you can't bring back the lights?" she asked.

The genius shrugged. "Probably not," he said. "But don't worry. Eventually the IT guys at the power company will get to the bottom of it. There's a lot of them. They can call in security guys from all over the world, not to men-tion the IT people at the equipment manufacturers. They would've found the malware by now, but they've hit the same roadblock. What they're probably doing is calling in reinforcements."

"I don't get it," Luis said. "They've got so much help, so many experts. Why are the lights still out?"

"You're not getting all that they have to do," Com-puter Genius said. "Just to identify the problem, they have to analyze the malicious code and decrypt it. After that, there's a whole reverse engineering process to see which of all those thousands of components it affects—not to mention what it does. It's like . . . it's like putting Humpty

Dumpty back together, get it? It'll probably happen, but it could take weeks."

Even in the bad light, Luis could see that Maura's face had gone pale. "Hampton will be a ghost town by then. People will move out if they can. Whoever's left will be desperate; they'll trash all the houses. It'll be one big dark, cold wasteland."

"Could be good for me, though," Computer Genius said. "More abandoned houses. Higher quality."

"Genius!" Maura said.

The genius pulled a wipe out of the box and used it to clean salt from his keyboard. "Of course," he went on, "if everybody's gone, who's gonna bring me my supplies? I guess there is, just maybe, one alternative."

Maura and Luis said, "*Yes?*"

The genius crumpled up the wipe and tossed it across the room. "There's more to this than code, you know. What if you guys play private eye? You know, like in the movies. How come you came to me in the first place? Did somebody give you a tip that a cyberattack caused the blackout?"

Luis looked at Maura, and she nodded—giving him permission. "Maura's grandfather," Luis said. "He used to work for the power company. We think he might know something, but he's sick. He can't really answer our questions."

"Try again," Computer Genius said. "Any kind of clue might help. I just need a little direction."

"You sound like Yoda," Luis said. "'Go forth, Luke Skywalker.'" Computer Genius ignored this.

"And there's one other thing. Whoever sabotaged the system probably left a back door for themselves."

"Uh . . . okay," said Luis, "meaning?"

"Meaning they're probably watching me prowl around the system myself right about now. They know somebody's onto them."

"Wait—do they know where we are?" Luis felt the hairs on the back of his neck stand up. Had the bad guys turned on the camera on the genius's laptop? Were all of them being watched?

"No way," said Computer Genius. "I mean, give me some credit. Even the IP address won't tell them much. All they know is it's somebody—and not the power company either. So you might want to keep that in mind." He pulled the covers up to his chin and yawned. "Come on back when you've got something helpful. The cash dollars you can leave in the coffee can."

CHAPTER TWENTY

Where did you get so much money?" Maura whispered as she and Luis picked their way down the stairs.

"Doesn't matter," Luis said. "Watch that step. See it? There's a hole."

"I'm *fine*," Maura said. "Where did you get the money?"

"I am being a gentleman," said Luis.

"You are being irritating!" said Maura. "Anyway, we're home invaders, not dinner guests."

"*Ouch*," said Luis. "Okay, fall through the floor if you want. See if I care. See if I notice."

"Thank you," said Maura. "I will."

On the second step from the bottom, Luis felt a chill. From every scary movie ever, he knew that ghosts and chills went together. It had something to do with ectoplasm. Not that Luis believed in ghosts . . . But now there did seem to be a *presence* in the house, a new presence.

Did Maura feel it too?

Luis did not want to ask. She would only make fun of him.

One final step down, and then Luis saw it—a ghost for sure, floating, *dancing* by the door. Luis stopped; he gasped; he raised an arm to protect Maura. His imagination ran away; he could not apply the brakes. He wanted to be a hero, wanted to be brave, but brave was not what he was feeling.

Then the voice of the ghost said, "Hello?" and Luis jumped. "Stay back, Maura!"

"Carlos?" Maura said. *"Finally.* Where were you?"

Luis's chest felt empty, and he took a breath to fill it. Did Maura know he'd been so scared?

Of course it was Carlos. Who else? The ghost was only the beam of a flashlight.

"Where you *been,* man?" Luis managed to keep his voice from squeaking.

"Here and there," said Carlos. Was Luis imagining it, or was he shaking? It was tough to tell in the bad light. "I ran into some guys. No phone. Did I miss anything?"

"You mean, like, *literally* ran into them?" Maura said. "You look upset."

171

"I'm fine," Carlos insisted.

"Did you bring the Advil?" Luis asked.

"Yeah, and a toothbrush too," Carlos said. "My mom keeps extras for tíos, you know."

"Are you sure you're okay?" Maura said.

"Leave me alone. Of course I'm sure," Carlos said. "Anyway, what do you care?"

"*Hey*—" Luis objected.

"I'm going upstairs," Carlos said. "Hasta luego—see you later."

It was dusk when Luis and Maura came out of 316 Larch. Luis took a deep breath of the sweet air and wondered if his body smelled like abandoned house. He was tempted to check his pits, but if Maura caught him she would never let him forget.

"What was up with Carlos?" Maura asked.

Luis shrugged. "Who knows? He's kind of a girl sometimes."

Maura frowned. "What's that supposed to mean?"

"Never mind," Luis said.

"I do mind," Maura said.

"So, okay, fine. You know. Delicate. Moody."

"Am I delicate? Am I moody?" Maura asked.

"Right now you're grouchy," Luis said.

Maura glared, and Luis cracked up.

"*What?*" Maura said.

"Is that what my fierce face looks like?" Luis asked. "Because if it is, it is most definitely scary."

CHAPTER TWENTY-ONE

Luis and Maura didn't have to discuss what they were going to do next. They both knew. They were going to jump on their bikes and head back to the hospital.

"Do we need a plan?" Maura asked as they set out.

"Save the day. Be the hero," Luis said.

"Not very specific," Maura said.

Luis stood up on the pedals. "I guess the plan is hope," he said, "like hope your grandpa is awake. Hope he can talk to us. Hope your mom might tell us something if he can't."

Anyway, they weren't going to give up, not while the lights were still out.

It was two miles to the hospital, a short ride on the level, empty streets. As he rode, Luis sensed something in the air, energy waiting to combust. He thought of the people behind the closed doors of their houses, people stuck in the dark and the cold. Were they getting ready to do something? Rise up and demand power the way Julia Girardo had said?

As the sky faded to black, the big city across the river shone brighter. When another light appeared ahead of them, Luis thought it was Whitman Hospital. Soon he realized he was wrong. This glow was yellow-orange and flickering—fire!

"It's on Main Street." Maura braked and slowed down. "It looks bad. Let's go left and go around it."

"Aw, come on. I wanna see," Luis said. "We won't stop. We'll just ride by."

Maura didn't answer, but she didn't turn either. A block away, Luis realized the building was the Rite Aid on the corner Fifth and Main. Sparks and flames shot through the roof, and ash swirled like dirty snowflakes in the air. In the parking lot, two cars and a Dumpster were also burning. The smoke stung Luis's eyes.

"Where are the fire engines?" Luis asked Maura.

"Around the corner maybe," she said. "Wait"—she looked around her—"what's going on?"

For an instant Luis didn't know what she meant. . . . Then he saw them too: shadows everywhere, moving fast in the firelight. Luis felt a chill—*I'm surrounded by ghosts!* But one bumped his bike, and he saw they were people, neighbors maybe, pumped up and almost crazy on a spree— pushing full shopping carts and carrying armloads of stolen clothes and shoes. One man struggled hard to haul a TV.

Luis felt fear but excitement too. Part of him wanted to join the fun. Who didn't want a new phone? Who didn't want new shoes? It was like Christmas only no one had to pay—you took whatever you wanted.

In the chaos, Luis had to jump off his bike or be knocked off. So much for not stopping. Maura had been right. They should have gone around. And now he realized the roar echoing in his ears was not only the fire but also whooping and shouting, far-away sirens, and something closer, a metallic *rat-a-tat-tat-tat.* . . .

Rocks? Bullets?

Jee-zus!

He called, "Keep your head down!" to Maura, whose head already was down. A few feet ahead of him, she was pushing forward behind her bike, staying low and aimed laser-like at the sidewalk on the far side of Main. If they just kept going, they would be okay, wouldn't they? But where was the fire truck? Why were there so few police?

In the flickering light, Luis's view was kaleidoscopic—here, a noisy crew trying to overturn a parked car; there, a guy smashing a fire extinguisher into a shop window; in the street ahead, a woman on her knees, hands over her face as if she'd been hurt.

Luis bent down. "Can I help—"

But the woman shook her head. "I'm okay, I'm okay." At the same time, someone tugged Luis's bike; someone else socked his arm. With an effort, Luis stayed on his feet, kept his bike, and continued moving.

This is a riot, he thought, *a riot in my own town.*

He had seen riots on TV—like that time after a cop shot a kid dead and left him in the street. But that had been somewhere far away, and this was here. He had bought Skittles and gum in that Rite Aid before. He had walked this block a zillion times. Now all at once it was changed. Would Hampton ever be the same?

Luis had almost made it to the far side of the street when—*RAT-A-TAT-TAT*—something hit his helmet, something hard that knocked his head to one side and hurt his face too—*ow!* What was it? Rocks? Gravel? He stayed on his feet, wiped his cheek with his fingers, realized his fingers were damp.

"Luis!" Now Maura was behind him. He tried to turn around, but someone twisted the handlebars of his bike hard. Luis lost his balance and sat down on the pavement. How did that happen? Where was the bike? Never mind—his tailbone hurt, and any second he might be trampled or run over.

"Are you okay? Get up!" Maura hooked an arm under his and yanked. Who knew she was that strong?

"My bike!" Luis said.

"Leave it—come *on.*"

"Oh, no." In the dark, Luis felt for the familiar shape, found it, lifted the bike, and pushed it ahead of him two-handed like a battering ram. He didn't think a single thought till he was safely on the other side of the street, shoved up against a building and panting. Finally, he caught his breath and looked at Maura. "Thank you."

To his surprise, she shrieked. "What happened to your face? There's blood all over you!"

"Never mind my face," Luis said. "My butt's the problem. I won't be sitting down for a while. Come on. Let's go visit your grandpa."

CHAPTER TWENTY-TWO

Amazingly, both bikes were okay. Luis and Maura rode the last block to the hospital without speaking. Luis's heart was still pounding, but the excitement faded along with the roar of the riot. Locking up his bike, Luis watched ambulances, red lights flashing, delivering injured people to the emergency room entrance at the other end of the parking lot. He hoped the lady on the street had gotten help.

Thinking of what he and Maura still had to do, Luis suddenly felt discouraged. How was a person supposed to stay brave in a frightening, terrible world? He wanted to say this out loud but couldn't think of the words.

"So many people hurt," Maura said, "including you, Luis. You should have somebody look at those cuts on your face."

"I'm fine," Luis said, but in fact both ends—his face and his butt—hurt a lot.

Inside by the TV, the crowd was bigger than usual. The news guys were saying that the riot in Main Street had started earlier in the day when someone at Julia Girardo's rally threw a rock at a police car.

Luis felt a pump of adrenaline: *We were there, center of the action.*

A middle-aged black man wearing blue scrubs glanced down and saw Luis's damaged face. "Ouch, son. What happened to you?"

"Not sure. I'm okay."

The man told him to go wash up. "You don't want an infection," he said. Luis thought he was probably a doctor. Anyway, washing up was a good idea.

Luis followed signs to a restroom on the ground floor. Only the emergency lighting was on, but when Luis looked in the mirror, he saw why Maura had squealed. There were dirt streaks and bloody pockmarks beginning to swell on his cheeks and chin. Luis couldn't help it; he tried out his fierce face and liked the effect.

There ought to be Halloween masks of me, he thought.

The soap dispenser was empty, but a few paper towels remained. Scrubbing got rid of the dirt but made the pockmarks raw, pink, and shiny. When Odysseus was injured fighting the Trojans, he must have looked like this. Maybe you had to suffer to be a hero.

Back in the lobby, Maura looked Luis over and winced. "Are you sure you're all right?"

"Let's go see your grandpa," Luis said.

It turned out that climbing multiple flights of stairs with a damaged tailbone was no joke. By the time they reached the sixth floor, Luis was hobbling, and Maura was trying not to laugh.

"I'm sorry," she said. "It's just you're usually so tough, and now—"

"Can we stop discussing my health, please?" Luis said.

"Right. Uh, Luis? Can we agree on one other thing?" Maura stopped in the corridor outside her grandpa's room.

"Yeah, what?"

"If Mom knows about the riot, knows we were there— she'll never let me out of the house again."

Luis shrugged. "So we don't mention it. That's cool." Maura nodded, but at the same time she was staring at Luis's battered cheek. *Talk about self-conscious,* Luis thought. *This is worse than zits.* "I'll say I fell off my bike. It's kind of true. Okay?"

"Okay," Maura said.

A second later they crossed the threshold of room 602 and got a surprise: Mr. O'Hara was sitting up. On a tray in front of him was a cup, a sandwich, applesauce, and two cookies packaged in cellophane.

"Grandpa!" Maura forgot Luis and hurried toward the bed.

"Hello." Maura's mom was sitting in a chair to the left of the door. Standing beside her, leaning against the wall, was Uncle Nate.

"Holy cripes, what happened to you, kiddo?" Uncle Nate asked.

Luis realized he was going to be answering this question a lot. "Fell off my bike," he said automatically.

"Onto your *face*?" Uncle Nate asked.

"I'm a klutz," Luis said.

Meanwhile, Maura was waiting patiently by the head of her grandfather's bed. Finally, he seemed to notice her and turned his head to look. Luis had a sinking feeling that his eyes would be blank, that he would not recognize his own granddaughter. He thought it would kill Maura if that happened.

But Mr. O'Hara did recognize her.

"Hello, honey," he said very quietly. Then he grimaced,

which might have meant that talking hurt his throat, or might have been his attempt to smile.

"Are you okay?" Maura asked him. "How do you feel? Do you want anything?"

To Luis, Mr. O'Hara looked as bad sitting up in bed as he had lying down. Maura's grandfather was always clean shaven. He got his hair cut every month. He wore neat, ironed clothes and shined shoes. Now there was a spot of soup or something on his hospital gown, his hair was uncombed, and there was gray stubble on his cheek. It was as if he'd been touched by an evil wizard's wand.

Maybe Maura was shocked too, but she hid it well and smiled. "You have to eat, Grandpa. Get your strength back."

"He wouldn't take a thing from me," Mrs. Brown said. "I hope you have better luck."

"How long have you been here?" Luis asked Maura's mom. "What does the doctor say?"

"Maybe an hour?" Mrs. Brown looked up at Uncle Nate, who nodded. "And the doctor came in for about fifteen seconds—long enough to say his alertness was certainly positive, but he's not out of the woods and they'll need to keep him another night."

Feeding Mr. O'Hara was a slow, messy process. It seemed obvious that he did want to please Maura, though, and he opened his mouth like a baby bird in a nature film.

A phone rang. The sound seemed to come from a lost world. At first Luis wasn't sure what it was. Then he realized the phone must be in Mrs. Brown's purse—it must be Grandpa's phone.

"Emily?" Uncle Nate said.

"Right. I forgot I had it." She took out the phone and looked at the screen. "Probably selling insurance—ha ha."

"May I?" Uncle Nate said, and—abruptly—took the phone from her and answered it.

The recorded voice was loud enough for Luis to hear: "This is card services . . . ." Luis had hung up on a hundred calls like it, but Uncle Nate didn't—or not right away. Instead he moved the phone away from his ear and studied the screen.

Mrs. Brown reached for the phone. "Nate?"

"Oh—uh, sorry." He hung up and handed it back. "Pops was always good with technology, way ahead of his time. I'm not surprised he's more comfortable with his phone than a lot of guys his age."

Mrs. Brown put the phone in her purse and spoke to

Luis. "My dad worked with technology his whole life, but he didn't have the advantages you kids have. He never went to college."

Luis saw his opening. "What was his job at NJL?"

"This and that over the years," Mrs. Brown said. "Before he retired, his last big assignment was replacing meters."

Boring, thought Luis. But he wanted to keep the conversation going. "Why did they do that?"

"The old ones were electromechanical, outdated technology," Mrs. Brown said. "The new ones are digital—smart meters."

Uncle Nate jumped in. "Pretty boring stuff for a kid, huh? Tell me about that bike accident. Bike okay? How are you going to get around?"

"Wait—what? Uh, sure. My bike's fine," Luis said. He was annoyed that Uncle Nate had interrupted, but he tried not to show it. He wanted to hear what Mrs. Brown had to say. "Uh, so sorry if this is dumb, but the electric meter—is that the thing with numbers on it on the wall in my basement? I never knew exactly what it was for."

"That's it," Mrs. Brown said. "Every customer has one, houses and businesses too. It used to be the meter had one simple job, keep track of how much electricity the customer uses every month. A meter reader came by to look at the dials and write down the numbers. Now it's all automated. The meter tells the billing department directly."

"The machine on the wall talks to the billing department?" said Luis.

"E-mails it more like," Maura's mom said. "The whole system's interconnected; every meter is part of it."

"This is all very dull—," Uncle Nate cut in again, but Mrs. Brown kept talking. Meanwhile, Maura encouraged her grandfather to eat. On the other side of the curtain in the shared hospital room, one member of the roommate's family remained sitting in a chair. She might have been reading a book or dozing.

"The smart meters are connected to one another and to NJL through the Internet," Mrs. Brown continued. "These days they do more than add up usage. If there's an imbalance of supply and demand—like when everybody's running their AC at once—the meters help keep us dispatchers informed so we can shift the load. Worst case, we can even shut down a customer's service—shedding load, it's called—to prevent a worse problem."

Luis's brain felt like a smart meter, one humming along at maximum speed, trying to process what it was hearing.

Could this be a clue—the clue Computer Genius needed?

"Earth to Luis?" Mrs. Brown was smiling.

"Oh, sorry," he said. "That's cool—interesting, I mean."

"You're a strange kid if you find that cool," Uncle Nate said.

Luis shrugged. "I like to know how things work."

"And you ask a lot of questions." Uncle Nate straightened his bow tie. "You better take care. You already got in one accident today. I wouldn't want all those questions to get you into trouble." Uncle Nate's expression was part grin, part something else.

What's he talking about? Luis wondered. *That was almost like a threat.*

Meanwhile, with Maura's patient prodding, Mr. O'Hara was eating more soup than he spilled. "Great job, Grandpa," she said over and over. "I am proud of you."

The nurse who came in a few minutes later offered to take the tray. "We are totally short-staffed," he said. "I'll be back in a sec. Then I'll need you visitors to clear out for a few minutes so I can check vitals and change that drip. How are you doing, Mr. O'Hara?"

Maura's grandpa turned his head slowly and looked the nurse in the eye. "I'm fine," he said.

"Me too," the nurse said. "Now if we could just get

this blackout over and done with. Mr. Bridgewater?" He looked at Uncle Nate. "Do you and the candidate have any kind of inside scoop?"

"You'd have to ask the incumbent mayor about that," Uncle Nate said. "I'm sure he's got it all under control— *not.*"

"What worries me," the nurse said, "is the hospital generator. It's designed for ninety-six hours—four days— and this is day two. After that, who knows? We'll have to move patients, and some of them may not make it."

Uncle Nate stood up. "Emily, I need to get back to work. If you want a ride home, I'll be happy to oblige, but we need to leave now."

"I'll see you later, Mom," Maura said. "Luis and I have some stuff to do—"

"Oh no." Mrs. Brown shook her head. "With all the crazies out there tonight? I want you safe at home."

Maura looked crushed, and Luis felt crushed too. Not that he needed Maura's help. He could handle whatever came next on his own. Still, it had been good to have a sidekick.

"Do you need a ride, Luis?" Mrs. Brown asked. "I wouldn't want your parents to worry either."

"To tell you the honest truth, I'm not sure I've got time—," Uncle Nate began.

"I'm totally fine," Luis said. "Honest."

"See you tomorrow," Maura told him. "Promise?"

"Promise," said Luis.

Mrs. Brown stepped toward the bed. "Dad, you have to stay here overnight. I hope you can come home tomorrow."

Mr. O'Hara didn't respond. He seemed to be staring at the blank TV, which hung from a bracket on the wall.

"Dad?" Mrs. Brown said.

"Okay," said Mr. O'Hara. "Bye-bye. Bye-bye, Nate."

"Oh!" Uncle Nate looked surprised. "I didn't think the old guy knew who I was. Bye-bye, Pops. You take care now."

CHAPTER TWENTY-THREE

Luis had a bad feeling about his sense of smell. He might be losing it. Otherwise, how to explain that walking into 316 Larch didn't seem so bad anymore?

"Genius?" he called. There was no answer, but that didn't mean anything. He turned on his flashlight and picked his way among the obstacles to cross the front room. An idea popped into his head. What would it be like to live here? Could you get the water working again? Clean it up? Paint? Bring in a generator? Bring in a refrigerator?

This would be after the new civilization rose up, the one based on the flea market by the ballpark.

Luis heard a grunt from upstairs, Computer Genius saying hello.

"Rise and shine!" he called, imagining Computer Genius still beneath the blankets. "Are you decent?"

This was something his father said to his mother sometimes. It meant: do you have clothes on?

"I have always thought so," came the answer. "There may be those who disagree."

By now Luis had learned that the sturdiest place to be on the stairs was on the outside, away from the wall. Keeping this in mind, he was able to move quickly. Midway to the top, he saw a glow coming from Computer Genius's room. Was it the laptop? It looked too bright . . . and it was.

When Luis entered, he was surprised. The genius was sitting cross-legged on a stack of folded blankets, head bent over a book in his lap. The genius looked different, better. He was wide-awake and well lit by half a dozen flashlights and one lantern. This was wasting precious battery power, but Luis didn't say anything. Something else was different too, a new smell—baby wipes.

When Computer Genius looked up, his face was clean. "What information do you bring?" he asked.

"I don't know if it will help," Luis said.

"Of course you don't," Computer Genius said.

"Mr. O'Hara was in charge of putting smart meters all over Hampton," Luis told him. "Could the blackout have something to do with that?"

Computer Genius nodded. "Possible, possible. What's a smart meter?"

Luis's heart sank. "Wait. You don't know?"

"Do you know?" Computer Genius asked.

"I do now," Luis said. "Mrs. Brown explained."

"But you only found out today," Computer Genius said. "So why would I know?"

Luis snorted. "Because you're Computer Genius! You're supposed to know everything."

"I didn't know about that Greek horse," Computer Genius said.

"That's just a story," Luis said.

"Some stories are important," Computer Genius said. "So tell the one about the smart meters."

Luis explained it the way Mrs. Brown had. Computer Genius caught on at once.

"Entirely possible," he muttered, more to his laptop than to Luis. "But I need more information. What kind of smart meters is NJL using?"

"The brand you mean?" Luis asked.

"And the model number," Computer Genius said.

"I don't know. How would I know?"

Computer Genius blinked but said nothing.

"I could go home and look at the one in our basement?"

Computer Genius blinked again.

"Or maybe there's one around this place somewhere."

Computer Genius shook his head. "Long gone for sure."

Luis was not happy. He remembered seeing the meter in the basement once. Where it was exactly, that was another question. "But why do you need to know the brand?"

"Bring back the information and I'll tell you. Oh, and one more thing. I need more money. Another two hundred will do."

"*Genius!* You know this is for the good of all of us— the whole town! It's like a public service you're doing!"

"If it's for the good of all, then all should pay," the genius said. "But what I've got is you, Luis. So you will have to pay."

Luis shook his head. Talking to the genius was like trying to hold on to water. Just when you thought you were getting a grip, it all drained away.

"All right," Luis said. "I'll be back as soon as I can."

The short bike ride home was quiet, dark, and eerie. Try as he might, Luis could not keep his heart from pounding anytime he saw a shadow coming out of nowhere. *I am being ridiculous,* he told himself. *This quiet is just quiet. There are no ghosts. Everybody has left town—the neighborhood is deserted.*

What about his parents? he wondered. Had they left too? Maybe some out-of-town tíos had come to fetch them. They would have had no way to let him know. He might get home and find nothing but a note.

"Mamá? Papá?" he called as he wheeled his bike into the cold, silent house.

"¡Aquí!" He heard footsteps, then felt rather than saw his mother come into the room. "Where have you been, Luis? We thought we were going to have to leave without you."

"Leave to where?" Luis asked.

"Wilmington," she said. "To stay with Tío Pepe. They have power there and gas in their car. We will come back as soon as this is over. There will be no work till then. I don't know what we will do for money. Your father is packing. You go pack too. Tío Pepe will be here soon."

"I'm not going," Luis said.

"No comiences, Luis—don't start with me. ¡Tú siempre molestas! You are always a pain! You can't stay home by yourself." Shaking her finger, his mother came toward him. When she got close, her eyes widened. "Did something happen to your face, Luis? Let me see!"

Luis stepped back. "I'm fine. Little bike accident is all."

"Were you wearing your helmet?"

"Sí, Mamá. Todo el tiempo. *Ow*—don't touch. There are bruises, but I'm fine."

His mom tried to get a better look, but Luis moved into the shadows. "I stay home by myself a lot. This won't be any different," he said. "Anyway, Reynaldo will be around, right? I have blankets and a flashlight, see?" He turned it on and aimed it in the direction of his mother's voice.

"Ay—get that out of my eyes! You're blinding me! Where did you get that? Did you steal it?"

Luis reaimed the beam at his mother's feet. The shadows of her calves made ink-black pillars on the wall. "Did you raise me to steal?" he asked.

"I certainly did not," said Mamá.

"Maura had extra flashlights, and she gave me one," he said.

"You are lucky in your friends," Mamá said. "But why must you stay?"

Because I am going to turn on the lights, Luis thought. *Because I can't leave Señora Álvaro's box.* Then he had an inspiration. "Computer Genius needs me."

"Computer Genius?" Like everyone else, his mom knew that name.

"He's living in one of the abandoned houses. Without me, he has no supplies. He'll freeze if he doesn't starve first."

"Are you taking him *our* food? It's not like we have extra," Mamá said.

Luis was out of patience. "I am staying here while you and Papá go to Wilmington," he said. "Reynaldo's not going anywhere. He'll make sure I'm okay—he always does. Besides, it's smart for someone to stick around our house. You know what happens to abandoned houses."

"And so you are a big man now defending our house? You are eleven years old, Luis," she said.

"I am eleven years old," Luis said, "and I am going to make you proud."

His mother sputtered something in Spanish—something about their mutual ancestors and the devil. Luis crossed in front of her and went into his own room. Even lit by the jittery beam of the flashlight, his four blue walls and sports posters comforted him. He wished he could hang out here for a while. He wished he had time to think and to rest up.

But he didn't. Later, when the lights were on and the bad guys—whoever they were—had been put away, then there would be time.

He felt for Señora Álvaro's box with his toe. It was there, and he bent down and opened it. The stale-lettuce money was still there too. From his parents' bedroom, he could hear his mother talking to his father. Luis did not want either of them to catch him with the box, so he grabbed two bundles of money, hoping it was enough, and stuffed them in his pocket.

Now to the basement, he thought. The doorway was in the kitchen, opposite the stove. At the top of the stairs, he flipped the light switch. When nothing happened, he cursed himself. Would he never get the hang of this?

Luis's parents did not keep a neat and tidy basement. What they did most of the time was drop useless or broken items from the top of the stairs and close the door quickly, like something might escape.

Luis made his way carefully down the stairs and then shone his flashlight in every corner of the room, moving it slowly so he didn't miss anything. He tried not to think about rats, spiders, cockroaches, and millipedes. He tried not to wonder what was growing in the dampness on the floor. The fact that he was used to abandoned houses did not seem to help in his own basement. After what seemed like a very long time, he spotted something protruding from the wall behind a broken chest of drawers full of baby clothes, something gray and made of metal.

Luis shoved a mattress out of the way, then leaned across two old kitchen chairs and trained his flashlight on the device. It was the meter, all right, and on it was a silver medallion: ITREX Model 2653589 MFD Toledo OHIO USA. Luis reached for his phone to take a picture, then remembered it was dead. He read the label twice, closed his eyes and recited it back to himself. *There. Got it.* At least, he hoped he did.

"Luis?" his mom was calling. "Are you in the basement?"

"Coming up," Luis said.

Climbing the stairs, Luis repeated the meter information to himself.

"Aquí estoy," he announced at the top. "And now I have to go."

His mom argued. "I don't know you anymore, Luis. You are *such* a big man. You think you don't need your parents. You think you are able to take care of yourself without help."

"Sí, por supuesto—of course." Luis retrieved his bike by the front door and turned to face his mom. He couldn't see her clearly. She was just another shadow. "I have to stay here in Hampton, Mamá. It is important. I will explain later. Can you trust me? I will see you after the blackout is over. Espero que sea muy pronto, very soon."

Someone else might have added, "I love you," but Luis had not said "I love you" to either of his parents since he was a toddler. It was Reynaldo who said those words—both to Luis and to his parents.

"Trust you?" His mother was sputtering again.

"Hasta luego, Mamá. Be safe."

Back on his bike, Luis stood up on the pedals and pumped. He was just getting used to the quiet when the sound of a car's engine disturbed it, the sound of a car close behind him. Why didn't he see headlights? Were the headlights turned off? Why would that be?

Luis could think of only one reason. Because someone was following him. And whoever it was did not want Luis to know.

But who would follow him, and why?

Luis got mad at himself for being paranoid, but the sound persisted. It was a good car, too, its motor purring smoothly. In this neighborhood, most of the cars were grumblers.

One more block and Luis thought he saw movement in the lot behind the chain-link fence. To get a better look, he stopped pumping and coasted. Now there was no doubt. A black figure ducked behind the weeds, then reappeared. Meanwhile, the car was still there.

Luis remembered something he'd heard in a movie, something about how it's not paranoia if somebody really is following you. Well, what if you thought two people were following you—one in a car and one on foot? What kind of paranoia was that?

He pedaled faster. Almost to 316 Larch, he had a thought. What if whoever it was wanted to know where he was going? What if whoever it was wasn't after Luis at all? Instead he was after Computer Genius? Was Luis leading him exactly where he wanted to go?

There was that backdoor thing the genius had mentioned. Had it given somebody a clue? Led them to Luis? Luis didn't see how that was possible, but then he didn't understand computers.

Luis felt like a rabbit pursued by a hunter. It was not a good feeling. *Think,* he told himself. *That is what heroes do—think clearly even when they're in danger. That is what makes a hero. If you are one, show it.*

CHAPTER TWENTY-FOUR

Luis had been in the abandoned house on Erie Street many times and knew it well. Computer Genius had squatted there for a while the winter before. It was an unusual house for the neighborhood because it stood by itself on a corner. Up until somebody decided to burn trash in the kitchen, it had been one of the better houses. Now it was less desirable.

Still, it was a place to hole up for a while. What did he care if it still smelled like smoke?

Luis locked his bike to a no-parking sign and headed for the porch. All the time, he tried to look casual, like a guy in no particular hurry. He didn't want his watcher to know that he was onto him.

Every abandoned house had its entry procedure. For the house on Erie, you levered a board off the front window—what had been the front window. Luis didn't happen to be carrying a crowbar, but when he turned on his flashlight he saw an old stick of lumber on the sidewalk. Careful to avoid nails, he grabbed it, shoved an edge under one of the boards, and worked to pry it off.

The stick was brittle and soon snapped. Luis looked around for another one and realized the engine noise was gone. Had the car driven away? Luis didn't think so. When he didn't hear a door open, he figured his watcher—his hunter—must still be inside.

There were no more sticks. Could he break down the door? How?

Think, Luis.

He had an idea. He removed his bike helmet, tugged to lengthen the strap, slid a section of it beneath the board on the window, and pulled as hard as he could.

Did the wood give? Maybe.

He tried again and—yes, for sure—the board was coming loose. Two more yanks and—*crack*—it broke.

Luis reached up, tore the dangling piece away, jumped for the hole it had created, leaned forward, and pushed his head and shoulders through. A moment later he landed awkwardly on his hands and knees. The floor was filthy, and he scrambled to his feet, his head immediately enveloped by a web of dust and bugs. He wiped his hands on his jeans, sneezed, wiped his nose on his sleeve. Even by the standards of an abandoned house, this one was bad. Luis turned on his flashlight and looked around. Every kid had a story about the worst thing they'd ever found in an abandoned house. Usually it involved the bodily functions of departed residents. Sometimes it was a passed-out resident himself. In fact, the appeal of exploring the houses wasn't really the chance of finding treasure. It was more the chance of finding something horrible, something worthy of a monster movie, something dramatic.

Now, though, Luis didn't need additional drama, and it was a relief when his flashlight found only trash and crumbling plaster.

Luis picked his way carefully over to the stairs and began to climb. The windows on the first floor were covered, but the ones on the second floor were not, and Luis aimed his flashlight toward the openings. Provided he was still paying attention, the hunter would see the flashlight up there and think—maybe—that Luis had come to stay for a while.

Now to fake him out some more.

Forgetting the state of his tailbone, Luis found a mostly clean spot on the floor and sat down—*ow!* He shifted to one side, then the other, trying to get comfortable, all the time ensuring that the beam from his flashlight stayed visible through the window. The cuts on his face hurt, and it was harder even than usual to stay still, hard to be patient. He wanted desperately to get back to Computer Genius. While he waited, he recited the information from the electric meter: ITREX Model 2653589 MFD Toledo OHIO USA.

Luis waited as long as he could stand it, then waited a little longer. He was just making a deal with himself—*five more recitations and I can get out of here*—when he heard a noise downstairs that made him jump.

What the?!

Luis thought for a split second, then turned off his flashlight. Having it on was like announcing his location. What should he do? Retreat upstairs to the third floor? But if he did, he might get trapped. Would jumping out a third-floor window kill him? Anyway, broken bones would slow him down.

The noise had come from the back of the house—somewhere near the kitchen. Someone definitely was inside, someone bumping and fumbling, someone without a flashlight, it seemed. Working flashlights were in short supply in Hampton.

Luis moved on tiptoe to the top of the stairs and looked down into darkness as black as a pit. Had the driver of the car circled around to the back and entered there? It would have been easier to follow Luis through the front window.

He heard another sound—not a *thump* but a *crack* from the front of the house. It sounded like wood splintering.

Two people had been following him. Now were they both inside?

Luis's heart began to pound. The tension was terrible, but a strange urge made him smile. The idea of the two hunters colliding in the dark was funny.

Then something truly surprising happened, something Luis had never counted on at all. Someone hollered: *"Luis—hey, Luis?"*

It was a kid, a familiar voice from the neighborhood. Luis couldn't identify it right away, and he never thought of answering. Safe in the dark, he intended to stay that way. He had to get back to Computer Genius. He had to protect himself. A few long seconds passed; then he heard another sound—this one terrible, the crack of something hard hitting bone, then a grunting, collapsing, depressing *unh* and the *thud* of a body hitting the floor.

Luis didn't know what had happened, but he knew one thing. He did not want it happening to him—and a flash of adrenaline flooded his brain. If he'd been right that calm under pressure made a hero, then never mind, he wasn't one. He for sure could not think now. He descended the stairs, two at a tumble, and tripped, nearly making a swan dive to the filthy front-room floor.

As it was, he grabbed what was left of the banister to catch himself, then landed sideways on his right ankle—*ow!* Add it to the injuries he'd already racked up that day, and keep going. He kept going. Operating on instinct, he made for what had been the kitchen. If one of the hunters had entered that way, then he—Luis—ought to be able to exit that way too.

Darkness, speed, and size were his allies, along with his knowledge of the house. He avoided the overturned toilet—there was an overturned toilet in every abandoned house—the splintered entertainment center, the perilous assortment of pipes and wires and cans of dried-up paint.

In the kitchen, the tiles had been swiped from the floor, and Luis moved carefully to keep from falling right through to the basement. The back door was in the corner, and he reached out blindly. The doorknob was gone—

usually they were—but the hole it left was something to grab. He yanked and the door opened. In the next instant, he slipped outside, jumped down to ground level, ran a few steps, and shouldered his way through the broken slats of an old, tumble-down fence.

He was in the alley, but not safe yet. Bad ankle, aching tailbone and all, he ran a block, cut through a vacant lot, then ran in the opposite direction. When he stopped, he listened, and the quiet was comforting. His heartbeat slowed; he took a moment to think.

Running through the house, he had felt a hostile human presence—the hunter still on his feet. It was only luck that Luis had evaded him. If he hadn't, he might have been knocked to the floor himself.

And who was the kid who had called his name? The kid was the one who had come in the back, and the other one—most likely the driver—had come in the front.

Luis imagined the voice again. *Luis—hey, Luis?* It was someone who knew him, but who? And why was he after Luis?

The next question that came to mind was unwelcome: *Is he okay?*

Luis tried to shake this off the way a dog shakes off

water. *I don't have time to be rescuing kids,* he thought. *The power is more important.*

While Luis had run a zigzag route, he still knew where he was—three blocks from Larch Avenue. He tested his ankle and started walking. He could get his bike in the morning. He'd gone only a short distance when he stopped. He was thinking of the kid lying hurt on the filthy floor, an unknown kid, but even so, Luis couldn't leave him there.

Crap. I have to go back. The people of Hampton can wait a little longer for their lights and precious televisions.

CHAPTER TWENTY-FIVE

Luis didn't return to the corner house directly. Instead, he circled around and approached from the other direction. His bike was still locked where he'd left it. He didn't see the hunter's car. Could he still be prowling the neighborhood? Could he still be in the house?

Not likely, Luis decided. *He was after me, and he knows I ran. He won't expect me to come back.*

Outside the window, Luis took two deep breaths, then jumped up, pulled, pushed, and wiggled his way between the boards. It was easier this time. The hunter must have been a big guy. Going through, he had enlarged the entrance. Inside, Luis switched on the flashlight, reluctantly casting off his protective cloak of darkness and revealing the hard ugliness of his trashed surroundings . . . which included the body of a kid lying in the dust on the floor.

Luis felt the breath rush out of his chest. Was he dead?

Luis knelt and aimed the flashlight. *"Hey,* wake up! ¡Levántate!"

The kid rolled onto his side and moaned. Not dead, then. And now that Luis saw who it was, he was just annoyed. He had come back to rescue *Tony Cencerro?*

"Hey," he said again. "You better be bad hurt, 'cause if you're not, I'll hurt you myself. What am I even doing here?"

"Luis?" Tony opened one eye. "Jeezus." He batted ineffectually at the flashlight. "Could you get that thing out of my face? What happened?"

Luis knew he was supposed to say, "That's what I want to know from you." It would be the next line on a show or in a movie. But the fact was Luis didn't especially care what Tony was doing there. Tony was a distraction. If he, Luis, was smart, he would abandon him again, leave right now.

"Get up," Luis said, but then he felt a little bad. "Can you?"

"What, hue—*no.* I don't know. My head hurts."

"Lemme see your face." Luis ignored Tony's protests and shone the flashlight into Tony's eyes. The pupils, which had been wide open in the darkness, constricted just like nature intended. "You don't have brain damage," Luis announced, something he had learned on TV. "Get up," he repeated, and this time he hooked his elbows under Tony's armpits and tugged.

More moaning. More groaning. Honestly, for a tough guy, this Tony was really a wimp. "Why are you making my life more difficult?" Luis asked as he struggled to lift Tony to his feet.

"Did somebody hit me?" Tony said. "Is that why my head hurts?"

"Yes, you dim bulb. Somebody hit you. I don't know who, so don't ask me. You can get home, right? There's a bump on your head but no blood. In my professional opinion, you are gonna live."

"I can walk home. *Jeez*, you don't have to be so rough," Tony said. "What's the hurry anyway? Wait—is the guy still here? The guy who hit me? I remember now. He was huge."

"Was he?" Luis tried to think of who he knew that was huge. Nobody came to mind. "He's gone," Luis said. "And I've got places to be myself."

"Listen to you." Tony attempted to reclaim some dignity. "The puffed-up eleven-year-old big man. *Hey*"—he got a good look at Luis for the first time—"what happened to your face?"

"You should see the other guy," Luis said. "Come on, I'll help you climb out."

Back on the street, Luis unlocked his bike with Tony watching and rubbing his head.

"I heard you were carrying cash," Tony said after a minute.

Luis looked up. "What?"

"Two hundred and fifty dollars. That's why I came after you," Tony said. "Plus I was mad about what happened at Señora Álvaro's bodega. I didn't like your attitude. I still don't."

"Yours could use improvement," Luis said.

"And Carlos said you were carrying cash," Tony went on. "So I thought, why not share and share alike."

Jeez, Carlos—¡imbécil! Luis thought.

"Uh, and how did this come up—the fact that I had money?" Luis asked.

Tony shrugged. "You might say I ran into him . . . a couple of hours ago. I asked him about your plans for the day. He was happy to share information. I guess I was pretty convincing."

"Did you hurt him?" Luis asked.

Tony shrugged. "Not really. I made it clear I could."

Suddenly Luis understood. Tony must have been the guy Carlos ran into earlier, the reason he was late getting to Computer Genius's. Luis felt a surge of anger at the universe and everybody in it—Tony, Carlos, the hunter, whoever had turned out the lights, Maura's grandfather. His face hurt. His butt hurt. He wanted to be home in bed like every other sixth grader. He wanted the streetlights and hot water back and the clock by his bedside table telling him the time. He wanted organic Pop-Tarts for breakfast. He wanted nothing to do with being a hero.

Still, when he spoke he kept his voice even. "I hope you're not expecting me to hand over any money now," he said.

Tony shrugged. "You didn't have to come back and help me. You know who knocked me out?"

"I think the guy was after me. I don't know who he is."

"Somebody who wanted your money?" Tony asked. Then he made a face. "My head hurts."

"Yeah, you said that. So go home—vete. The walk'll be good for you. I saw somewhere you're not supposed to go to sleep right after you get hit on the head."

"I owe you," Tony said.

"Verdad," said Luis. "Buenas noches."

Luis's bike was unlocked and ready to go, but now he hesitated to jump on. If the hunter came back, he'd see it was gone and know Luis had come back for it. *Heck with him,* Luis thought. *I need my wheels.* A few minutes later, he rode up to 316 Larch, locked the bike to the railing, and hurried inside.

"Genius?" he called as soon as he'd pulled the door closed. "Are you decent?"

"Some would say so," came the reply.

trex—I-T-R-E-X." Computer Genius typed it into search.

"Aren't you curious about my face?" Luis asked. "Don't you want to know where I was? There was this hunter guy, and he knocked out Tony, and—"

Computer Genius looked up from his computer. He was frowning. "Do we need to talk about this now?"

"Uh, I guess not," Luis said. "I just thought—"

"I have a job to do," Computer Genius said.

"Okay." Luis had thought he was tired of people asking about his face, but the genius's lack of interest was disappointing. Wasn't he important too? But maybe he wasn't, not at this moment. "So, uh, what are you going to do next?"

"I studied up while you were gone," the genius said, still tapping away at his laptop. "Smart meters communicate with each other. And they communicate with the operations center at New Jersey Light too—only in that case, the communication goes both ways. Pretty regularly, the ops center sends the meters software updates, same as you get on your home computer. And the meters accept the updates, reconfigure themselves, and go on doing the job. Do you get my drift?"

Luis thought for a second. The adrenaline shot was over. He felt tired and dull. He yawned. "No," he admitted.

"Can you stop yawning?" the genius asked. "It's distracting."

"Sorry," Luis said.

"Do you *want* me to explain?" the genius asked.

Luis nodded.

"All right, then," the genius said. "So I think what happened here is our hacker hooked the NJL server and dropped in an update of his own. The server sent it out to the PLC—"

"PLC?" Luis repeated.

"Programmable logic controller. It's like a simple computer designed for a particular job—like talking to electric meters. The PLC relayed the software update to the meter. This one didn't tell the meter how to add up the billing or the kilowatt hours; it said something else. It said—"

"—shut off the power," Luis said.

The genius pointed at Luis's nose. "Got it. I guess you're not as dumb as you look."

"Gracias," said Luis.

Computer Genius ducked his chin, a nod of approval. "Then one by one by one by one, obedient little meters here, there, and everywhere did as they were told."

Luis shook his head. The idea was freaky—a harmless gadget in your house going rogue. "It's like your microwave attacks you, or your fridge," he said. "I never knew it was possible."

"Get used to it," the genius said. "Cars talk to the Internet too, you know."

Luis shook his head. "Don't tell me that, hue. I don't even want to think about that."

"Yeah." The genius looked back at the screen and hit enter. "I'd stick to a bike if I were you. Okay—here we go. Look at this. Is that it?"

Luis leaned in to look at the genius's laptop. On the screen was a photo of an electric meter. "Yes," he said.

"The model numbers match," Computer Genius said. "Let's see if I can find the manual."

A few key strikes later, a PDF file appeared—page after

page of small print describing the inner life and working of the ITREX 2653589.

"I'll just search remote disconnect relay"—the genius narrated his actions—"and when I find it, maybe I can identify the relevant lines of code."

"And reverse the command?" Luis said.

"Depends on how smart our hacker was," the genius said. "We can only hope it's gonna be that simple. Go ahead and get comfortable. This may take a while."

Copying the genius, Luis sat himself down cross-legged on the floor. Up till this point, he had been too focused on the job to look around. Now he did—and he was astonished. It had been only a few hours since he and Maura and Carlos had found Computer Genius holed up in the dark and the cold and the grime, right? But in that time the space had transformed.

The mattress had been plumped, sheets shaken out, blankets folded. Remnants of curtains hung over the windows. If you squinted, you could pretend the tatters were lace. The toothbrush Carlos (that traitor!) had supplied stood upright in a jam jar on the windowsill.

Was Luis imagining it? Or did he smell mint?

In daylight, the leftover streaks, stains, and crumbs

might have revealed themselves, but for now—in the forgiving glow of lanterns and flashlights—the place looked downright homey.

Luis turned his focus back to the genius and got another surprise. The formerly scraggly hair had been pulled back and secured with a more-or-less clean bandana. The face and hands were clean, the T-shirt tucked neatly into the plaid pajama bottoms. All the genius lacked was a bow tie.

Luis knew better than to comment. The genius was deep in concentration, and for a few minutes the only sounds were clicking keystrokes. Had the genius cleaned up because he had work to do? He remembered the comment about being in hibernation. Well, the genius wasn't hibernating now.

Luis, in contrast, had nothing to do, so he gave in to exhaustion and dozed. What finally woke him was the quiet when Computer Genius stopped typing. Luis opened his eyes and saw him pulling off his headphones, rubbing his ears, lolling his head to stretch his neck.

"The guy's not even that smart," the genius said. "I'd be embarrassed if my hack was that kludgy. The man-in-the-middle part, though, that was pretty good."

"Man-in-the-middle?" Luis repeated. "What guy?"

"Whoever did the actual hack. I think I might know the kid. Hacking circles aren't that big, you know. And every hacker has his own digital fingerprint."

"What do you mean?" Luis asked.

"Particular lines of code they like to use, ways of doing things," the genius said. "The man-in-the-middle was a nice touch, like an add-on."

"You know I have no idea what you're talking about," Luis said.

"Of course I know," Computer Genius said.

"So would you mind enlightening me?" Luis asked. "Por favor."

"Okay, since you said 'please,'" the genius said. "Our bad actors, they wanted to keep their interference a secret as long as possible, give the outage time to take off. So they set up their malware to make a copy of normal operations and then, when the time came, play the copy back on the monitors being watched by dispatchers in the operations center."

Luis understood at once. "I saw something like that in a movie," Luis said. "Robbers broke into a bank, but they fixed the security monitors so they played a videotape of the empty vault instead of the real picture from the cameras, the one that showed them stealing the money. To the guards looking at the TV screen, it looked like everything was fine."

"Same idea," Computer Genius said. "The operators thought it was a normal day."

Luis remembered something else. "They're not called 'operators.' They're called 'dispatchers,'" he said. "That's Maura's mom's job, and she got in trouble because she didn't see the outage as it happened."

"It wasn't her fault," Computer Genius said. "It was part of the plan."

"But wait—" Luis shook his head to clear the drowsiness. "Does that mean you fixed it? Are the lights on?"

"I'm still working on it," Computer Genius said. "Can't a guy take a break?"

"Sure," Luis said. "Sorry."

"Somebody on the inside must have provided the bad guys with the encryption key so they could read the data on the meters," he said. "The easiest way would have been to give over one of the NJL technicians' laptops. All the information is in there. The meters are such a big attack surface—it's almost surprising nobody has tried this before."

"Maybe nobody wanted to turn out the lights before," Luis said.

The genius nodded. "That could be it exactly. Why turn out the lights in a Podunk town like this? It makes no sense. There's no military base here. No giant corporation to pay big money to get back in business. There's just a bunch of people like you and me. Who even cares enough to shut us down?"

Luis started to answer, but the genius wasn't really listening. He had more to explain.

"A lot of these old systems were set up before there was even an Internet," the genius said. "There was no thought that somebody could be trying to hack them because there was no way in, no network. But in today's world, where everything's connected, it didn't take a lot of smarts to hack into the system. Communications between the server and the PLC weren't encrypted, so the hacker could see the sent commands, copy them, then substitute his own."

The genius took a breath before returning his headphones to his ears. "Back to it," he said.

Luis had always been impressed by the genius. Now he was in awe. All that reading lines of code, all that hard thinking to decipher what it meant—he wondered if he would ever have that much patience for anything.

On the other hand, wasn't he—Luis—demonstrating

awesome patience right now? All this waiting was killer, especially with his tailbone in its current state, especially without a phone.

When another half hour passed, Luis began to worry that—awesome as he was—the genius would never find the problem. If he couldn't, would there be weeks without power? Would everyone clear out and abandon their houses? What about school?

Maybe he, Luis, would have to go live in Wilmington with Tío Pepe, start school in a new place. Maybe Hampton really would become a ghost town. Maybe a new civilization would rise. Had that been the bad guy's plan all along?

Had Luis read too many comic books?

Who was the bad guy, and what did he want? Luis was so engrossed by his thoughts that it took him a moment to notice when something made a noise downstairs. Wait . . . what? Had someone tripped? Someone large?

Who could it be but the hunter?

CHAPTER TWENTY-SEVEN

Luis could have kicked himself for his stupidity. The genius had lit the room with lanterns and flashlights—light easily visible from the street. As if that weren't enough, Luis's bike was locked out front.

We should have just put up a sign, Luis thought. *Hunter: We're here!*

With his headphones on, Computer Genius hadn't heard the thumps. He was still the model of concentration. Luis opened his mouth to tell him, then didn't. *This is my job,* he thought. *Protect the genius; let him finish his work.*

Luis rose from the floor, moved quietly to the bedroom doorway, and peeked out, careful to remain hidden. Once, when the house was lived in, there would have been a railing around the stairwell. That was gone now, and all that remained was the opening, a hole, a sheer drop to the stairs and the ground floor below.

The hunter knows we're up here, Luis thought, staring

into the darkness. *He's going to come up and get us.*

Luis thought of Tony, who had gotten in the hunter's way and been knocked out for his trouble. The hunter must have assumed that Tony was Luis, then realized that he wasn't, that the real Luis was running out the back door. *I'm what he wants, but why? And why is he hanging around down there? Why not come up and face me?*

It wasn't long before Luis got his answer. Only he didn't see it as an answer at first. Instead, it was one additional bad smell among all the others. The next clue was a faint glow that brightened till it cast dancing shadows on the wall ahead of him. The glow didn't come from Computer Genius's room. It seemed to come from somewhere on the ground floor.

Does he have a lantern? Luis thought. *He didn't have one before.*

Finally, there was a noise—a crackle, and along with it still more shadows, shadows that momentarily became wisps of smoke.

"Got it!" Computer Genius hollered, triumphant.

"Fire!" Luis spun around to face him. "There's a fire downstairs. Get up—we gotta go!"

Computer Genius didn't understand at first. With a big

grin on his face, he pulled off his headphones and started to explain exactly what he'd done. But Luis wasn't listening. He rushed over, manhandled the genius to his feet, and shoved him toward the window. Already the floorboards were warm.

"Hold on to your laptop," Luis said. "Everything else we leave."

Computer Genius started to argue, but he must have smelled the smoke. His face turned first blank, then terrified. "What do we—," he started to ask.

Honestly, Luis didn't know. *We're toast,* he thought, only for once it wasn't funny. Go downstairs, they'd go into an oven. But soon the floor they stood on would collapse. If they went upstairs it would buy some time, but would it be enough? Like the cops, the firefighters were busy. An abandoned house would not be top priority.

Luis thought all this through in a flash and made the only decision possible: "Window," he said, and shoved the genius toward it.

The air in the room warmed up and the smoke became a presence that stung your eyes and hurt your chest. It was all happening fast. It was keep up or give in. Luis tugged the curtains down, ignoring sharp edges and nails, then yanked the battered old sheets of plywood free.

"Go!" He shoved the genius toward the opening.

"Wait!" Computer Genius protested.

"No time!" Luis kneed him in the butt, and the genius lurched into the night. "Grab a branch!" Luis commanded. The genius did so and let go of the laptop. Luis lunged for it and made a lucky catch. *Save and a beauty,* he thought, climbing out the window himself and grabbing on to a twisted branch.

Luckily, the branch he chose was sturdy. Gripping it, he swung forward till his right foot gained purchase on a lower branch close to the trunk. He let go, fell forward, lost his balance, and dropped into thin air before his desperate fingers found still another branch, which prevented his crashing to the sidewalk. Miraculously, the laptop remained under his arm.

Computer Genius, meanwhile, had not descended from his original perch, the branch nearest the second-floor window.

"¡Necesito ayuda! Help me!" he called.

Luis dropped to the sidewalk and looked back. "Okay, genius," he said. "Your turn to follow instructions." Then, toehold by toehold and grip by grip, he began the process of talking his friend down. Luis was surprised that he could see the genius clearly among the branches of the tree. Was it dawn already? Or was the fire casting that much light?

At last, panting and sweaty, the genius dropped to the sidewalk. "Gracias," he said. "I'm not sure, but maybe you saved my life."

"I got you into this. I had to get you out," Luis said, and then remembered they weren't really out yet. Where was the hunter?

Luis looked away from the house, scanning the street and the sidewalk till, sure enough, something in motion caught his eye—a big man lumbering bearlike down the block, bald head gleaming in the glow of streetlights. Luis thought the man seemed familiar. Then Luis thought something else.

Wait a second. *Streetlights?*

Luis looked up and saw to his astonishment that a couple of them were lit, and then, as he watched, others began buzzing to life as well. There were a few occupied houses on this block of Larch, and two porchlights came on. Then—oh, wonderful noise—he heard the blare of voices from TVs.

"Genius?" Luis said, looking him in the face.

Computer Genius shrugged. "Yeah. I thought that last code was gonna work. And you want to know something funny? The file that turned out the lights was called 'zap.exe.'"

By this time flames were licking the window frames, and the outside air was smoky. In the distance, Luis heard a siren. "We gotta go, Genius," he said. "I have a feeling things might get complicated if we stick around."

CHAPTER TWENTY-EIGHT

For Luis, the sound of the six a.m. alarm had never been so sweet.

He sat up in bed, batted the clock to shut it up, and then regarded the time. The illuminated numerals, 6:01 a.m., looked cheerful. So did his phone when he unplugged it and stared at the colorful, bright, useful icons on the screen. He thought he had never appreciated their beauty till now, or the fact that the lights would turn on when he flicked a switch. He might make oatmeal in the microwave for the sheer thrill of making oatmeal in the microwave. From the kitchen came the hum of the fridge, and it was a beautiful noise.

Computer Genius was curled up in a nest of sheets and blankets on the floor. His head rested on his laptop. Luis had offered him a bed, but he refused to take it or the sofa either. So much comfort, he had said, would only make him uncomfortable.

Luis stepped over Computer Genius, dressed quietly, then pushed his toe under the bed to make sure the box was still there. It was, and he went into the bathroom and washed his face—isn't hot water a wonderful thing?—then to the kitchen, where he turned on the TV news.

Naturally, the reporting was all about the end of the blackout—the multimillion-dollar hit to the local economy, the traffic jams as residents returned, lines at reopening gas stations and grocery stores, business owners cleaning up the mess left by looters and filing insurance claims. The scale of the damage was only now being added up.

The newscasters themselves seemed giddy with relief. *I feel ya,* Luis thought.

But how had the power been restored? What had been the problem in the first place? The newscasters didn't say. All agreed it was a surprise when the power came back on. There had been no hint about that during New Jersey Light's last press conference the night before. Another press conference was scheduled for the afternoon. They expected more information then.

A commercial came on—that election ad where the lady running for mayor, Julia Girardo, makes the baby cry. Luis laughed even though he'd seen it a million times.

Anyone who frowned at a baby that way had to be a terrible person—but hadn't Maura said her uncle Nate worked for her? *Grown-ups are weird,* thought Luis.

He stirred water and the contents of an oatmeal packet in a bowl, wondering how much the people at the power company knew. Could they identify Computer Genius's laptop as the one that had been poking around their system? Could they use GPS to identify its location—the genius's location? When the truth came out, maybe the genius would get prize money, or a medal, or free electricity for life.

Maybe I will, too, Luis thought. *I wouldn't mind being celebrated. Maybe it would help me get girls. Not that I want girls exactly, but Reynaldo says someday I probably will.*

But wait—no. What was he thinking? To claim his share of glory, Luis would have to reveal the part about Mr. O'Hara. He had helped the bad guys—whoever they were—but he was sick and he was Maura's grandfather. No way could Luis rat him out, and if Computer Genius wanted to take credit, he would have to leave both Luis *and* Maura's grandpa out of the story.

Luis was pretty sure Computer Genius could be

counted on to do that. Unlike some people (Carlos!), he was not a blabbermouth.

Oh, well, Luis thought. The coolest superheroes were always the ones who operated in secret. Even Odysseus had disguised himself when first he came home from the war.

Luis ate the sweet warm oatmeal standing at the kitchen counter. Between bites he texted Maura. **Hey, sup? How's grandpa? U? Lots to tell. I have questions! Do u have answers?**

Maura must not have been up yet because there was no reply.

Besides talking to Maura, Luis had one other priority: money. He could explain all day to Señora Álvaro that he had borrowed four hundred and fifty dollars to pay the genius to fix the computers and fix the blackout. He could explain all day—and Señora Álvaro would only raise one eyebrow and hold out her hand. Luis would have to find a way to pay her back.

Luis was pondering this problem when Maura replied: **Come over right now,** followed three seconds later by a second text: **Please.**

• • •

Luis left a note on the genius's pillow telling him to text when he woke up. Then he texted his mom to say don't worry about the kid asleep on the floor. Like everyone, his mom knew the legend of Computer Genius, but she had never seen him in the flesh. **He's harmless**, Luis wrote.

Luis's mom didn't answer. Maybe she was still asleep. Way down in Delaware—did his parents even know the power was back?

The morning was clear and warmer than the day before. The good weather matched the good mood of a city returning to normal, a city with electricity and gasoline and heat and precious television. *You'd almost think we were civilized or something*, Luis thought.

Halfway down the block on his bike, whom should he see but Carlos walking up the sidewalk in his direction.

Carlos the snitch. Carlos the traitor. Carlos, his cousin and former friend.

"You're not dead," Carlos said when Luis stopped in front of him. He wasn't kidding either. His face showed obvious relief.

"No thanks to you," Luis said.

"Wait—you know about that? I mean . . . I mean . . ." Carlos stammered in confusion.

Luis was in a hurry. Whatever Maura wanted couldn't wait. Still, he was curious how Carlos planned to explain himself. So he put on his most innocent face and asked, "Know what?"

"Nothing," Carlos said quickly.

"Am I *supposed* to be dead?" Luis asked.

"Never mind that," said Carlos. "The electricity's back. ¡Qué bueno! What did you have for breakfast? I had waffles."

"I'm surprised you tore yourself away from World of Warcraft long enough to come over here," said Luis. "You must've really been worried."

"Is Computer Genius okay?" Carlos asked. "I heard sirens last night, and then I heard there was a fire in one of the old houses. It wasn't the one on Larch, was it?"

"Sí," said Luis.

Carlos had been doing a good job controlling his face, but now he failed. He looked hit in the nose, as if he might cry. "Dios mío," he murmured. "Is he okay? Is he the one who fixed the blackout?"

"Let me ask you something," Luis said. "When was the last time you saw Tony Cencerro?"

When Carlos caved, he didn't mess around. Luis had

to give him that. All at once, the story came tumbling out, pretty much exactly the way Tony had told it, only interrupted by a lot of "I'm so sorry" and "I'm so rotten." Luis listened till he got bored, which wasn't very long.

"Shut up," he said finally.

Like a balloon deflating, Carlos sputtered a little longer. Finally, he asked, "What are you gonna do to me?"

"Don't know yet. Stand by. Gotta go," Luis said.

"Where?" Carlos asked.

"Like I'd tell *you*," Luis said. Then he stood up on the pedals and took off.

It seemed to Luis as he rode that everyone he passed was smiling. Neighbors were talking together on the street. Even in the long lines for gas, people were out of their cars, clapping each other on the back, and laughing. It was like the best holiday ever. Tomorrow people would go back to work, Luis would go back to school, and everyone would be frowning again. But now it was time to celebrate. The world hadn't ended. The lights were on. Normal had never looked so good.

The sunshine and the chilly breeze were exhilarating. Luis's brain worked to the fast rhythm of bike pedals pumping. Who had caused the blackout in the first place, and why? Who was the hunter? How was he connected to the blackout—or was he? *More likely it was someone else like Tony,* Luis thought, *someone who knew I had money on me. I should've asked Carlos if he talked to anyone else. Or could it be Tony who blabbed?*

Passing the mall, Luis saw that some of the TV trucks had packed up already, but the ones from nearby stations were still there. Julia Girardo's pickup truck, the one covered in her campaign signs, was in the lot too.

Luis was coasting fast when he got to Maura's turnoff and leaned hard to make the right. It was too bad Tony didn't remember anything that happened right before he was hit in the head, too bad he couldn't describe the hunter's face. Luis thought back to how the big bald guy running down the street had seemed familiar, even from behind. It could be he had seen him before. It wouldn't be that strange. Hampton was a city but a small one.

At Maura's front door, Luis pulled out his phone and texted: **I'm here!**

When Maura answered the door, she didn't smile. Instead she took a deep breath.

"Are you okay?" Luis asked.

She nodded but wasn't very convincing. "I think so, but I'm glad you're here."

"What happened? I've got a lot to tell you. You will never believe it. Is your grandpa home?"

"He came home this morning. Now he's back at his place, resting. My mom's there with him," Maura said. "Everything is probably fine, but I'm kind of freaked out. It's good the power's back. Did that just happen like normal, or did . . . you know . . . Computer Genius?"

Now that the heat was back, they sat down at the kitchen table to talk. Luis was not one for unnecessary details. If he hadn't been interrupted, he could have told the whole story in five minutes. But Maura asked a lot of questions and made a lot of comments of her own. They were twenty minutes in by the time Luis described the hunter in the streetlights.

"Does that sound familiar to you—big bald guy, kind of slow on his feet?" Luis said.

Maura shrugged. "You only saw him from the back, right?"

"There was something about him . . ." Luis shook his head. "Anyway, that's pretty much the whole story. I rode by 316 Larch this morning. A fire truck was still there, and the guys were cleaning up. The front of the house doesn't look that bad, but it's all black around the windows. I bet the insides are burned out."

"You could've died," Maura said. "Did you think of that? Was this hunter guy trying to kill you?"

"I don't know," Luis said. "Maybe he just wanted to scare us. Anyway, he saw us get out. I think he must've waited around till we did. He only ran when the lights came on."

"You have to tell the police," Maura said.

"I don't know," Luis said. "I don't want to tell them about your grandpa."

Maura was still for a minute. "I hadn't thought of that. Maybe tell the police but skip the part about how my grandpa might be involved?"

Luis nodded. "But if they investigate? If they find the bald guy and there's some connection between him and your grandpa?"

"How could that be?" Maura asked.

Luis shook his head. "I don't know. I don't know who the hunter even is. But we need to think before we say anything."

Maura nodded. "I guess you're right."

"Anyway, what did you want to tell me?" Luis asked. "When I got here, you looked like you'd seen a ghost—freaked out, you said. What is it?"

"Maybe I'm being a girl the way you always say," Maura said. "But here it is. I rode in the backseat with my grandpa when Mom brought him home. Mostly I thought he was asleep, but all of a sudden about halfway home, he opened his eyes and looked right at me. You said I looked scared? He really looked scared—like having a nightmare only awake."

"Did he say 'zap' again? Or a number?" Luis asked.

Maura shook her head. "Nothing like that. What he said was: 'Be careful. You and Luis both. Promise me.'"

Luis felt a pang in his chest. Was he freaking out a little too? "Did you ask him what he meant?"

Maura nodded. "Yeah, but he didn't say. He just said, 'Promise me,' again. So I did."

"Your mom was there. She was driving. What did your mom think?" Luis asked.

"She couldn't see his face, how scared it was. She didn't think it was that important. She said it was maybe his meds."

Luis and Maura were speculating about what

Mr. O'Hara might have meant when the sliding doors from outside opened, and Mrs. Brown came in.

"How's he doing, Mom?" Maura asked.

"Sleeping," Mrs. Brown answered. "Hey, Luis. How are you? I came back to get some decent coffee. The stuff my dad keeps in his apartment is swill. Isn't it glorious to have electricity again?"

"And another day off school," Luis said.

"Speaking of which, I hope they call me back to work soon."

"I hope so too, Mom," said Maura.

"Nate said yesterday that he'd put in a good word if I needed him to. He still has connections at NJL—even though he hasn't worked there in years."

"Now he works for that lady who's running for mayor?" Luis said.

"The woman, yes," Mrs. Brown said. "She's not my candidate, though. She got people even more riled up over this blackout. It made things worse."

Luis remembered seeing her truck at the mall.

"Hey, Mom," Maura said. "Do you think it's okay that Grandpa stays over at his place by himself? I could give him my room."

"You're a good kid, Maura," Mrs. Brown said. "But I set up his phone so he can dial me with one keystroke. That he can manage. Like Nate said, 'Pops was always good with technology.'"

Maura smiled. "I think it's funny that Uncle Nate calls Grandpa 'Pops.'"

"I don't know where he got that. No one else uses it," her mom said.

Something poked Luis's brain—something that had to do with the hospital yesterday. Mrs. Brown had been telling him about the smart meters, and Uncle Nate kept interrupting—said Luis would get in trouble if he kept asking questions. Hadn't it almost seemed like a threat? Then he said that thing about Pops and technology.

And later—last night—a big guy driving a nice car had gone hunting for Luis.

What if there was a connection?

"Maura," Luis said. "What's your uncle Nate's last name?"

"Bridgewater," she said.

"That's right," Luis said. The nurse had said it at the hospital. "Nate Bridgewater," he repeated, "NB."

Maura looked puzzled. "Uh, sure. So what?"

Luis took a breath. He might be crazy. But he didn't think so.

"Mrs. Brown," Luis spoke slowly, "do you happen to know when Mr. Bridgewater's birthday is?"

Maura's mom made a face. "That's an odd question, Luis, but I do, actually. My birthday's on Valentine's Day, and we used to talk about what a pain it is to have a holiday birthday. His is New Year's Eve."

"Why—," Maura started to ask, but Luis was on his feet.

"We gotta go," he said. "I mean, that is—Maura, can you come with me? Is that okay, Mrs. Brown? We're not going far, just to the mall. And our phones are charged. You can call us if you need help, or if Mr. O'Hara does."

"Are you okay?" Mrs. Brown asked. "You have a strange expression on your face."

"It's his fierce face, Mom," Maura said.

"Sorry," Luis said. "I'm fine. Muy bien. Never better."

"If you say so, and I guess I can spare Maura for a while. Maybe later you can take a shift with your grandpa? For now—provided I get a cup of decent coffee—I think I've got it covered."

Luis pulled out his phone as he and Maura headed for the door.

"What is the big hurry?" she asked. "Who cares when Uncle Nate's birthday is? Who the heck are you texting?"

"Backup," Luis said. "Because if Julia Girardo is still at the mall, we are going to need it."

CHAPTER TWENTY-NINE

t was ten o'clock when Luis and Maura rode their bikes into the mall parking lot. Only three TV trucks remained. Deprived for two days of their retail fix, desperate shoppers had begun to stream in and fill the lot. The lights were on, and soon the cash registers would be too.

Meanwhile, Julia Girardo's political extravaganza in a pickup had moved to a plot of asphalt near the highway. Now that the people had other diversions, the candidate had attracted only a small crowd, but her amplified voice carried everywhere.

On the short bike ride from her house, Maura had asked Luis at least five times what was going on. "You'll see," Luis kept answering. "Everything's gonna be fine."

"Of course it's gonna be fine. The lights are back on. Why wouldn't it be fine?" Maura sounded worried.

"You'll see," Luis said.

Less than five minutes after Luis and Maura rode into the lot, Tony and his squad arrived too, and they were noisy about it. They were not on bikes but on motorcycles and in old cars. For night birds who usually woke up at noon, their efficiency was impressive.

"Is this what you meant by backup?" Maura asked.

Luis nodded.

With one exception, the guys looked remarkably alike—they wore tight jeans and black jackets embroidered with skulls and other symbols. Their hair was pulled back and shiny. They had scruffy goatees on their chins. Only one kid looked different. He emerged from the backseat of a Ford Galaxy. He had a baby face and wore khakis and a Phillies cap.

It was Carlos.

Carlos did not ordinarily run with Tony's crowd, but Luis had asked Tony to pick him up on the way. Now Carlos spotted Luis across the hood of the car and gave him a wordless, *What gives?*

Luis answered with a shrug that meant "You'll see."

But Luis's cool was 90 percent for show. *This is my chance to be a hero,* he was thinking, *or to mess up big-time.*

Meanwhile, Julia Girardo droned on: "Carnage . . . strength . . . losers . . . take back . . ." It was the same stuff she'd been saying right after the blackout began. Now Luis wondered if Uncle Nate—Nate Bridgewater—had written these words for her.

"Are we ready, boss?" Tony came up.

Maura's eyes widened. Luis knew what she was thinking and tried not to gloat. Tony had called him "boss." Sure, it was partly a joke. But there was some truth to it too. Not that this was going to last, but for now at least the big kid was taking orders from an eleven-year-old.

"It's the guy driving the truck." Luis indicated with his chin. "Don't let him see you yet. It's fine if he sees the crew, though."

"We are on it." Tony made a sharp, almost military gesture. His troops fell in behind. Together they began a slow and apparently casual advance toward the pickup truck. Carlos, after a last baffled look at Luis, went with them.

"*What*—," Maura started to ask for the millionth time.

Luis suppressed a nervous grin. "Come with me," he said.

Julia Girardo by this time had cycled into the question-and-answer portion of her spiel, the part that gave her the slogan that made her popular. Had this been Nate Bridgewater's idea too?

As Luis and Maura approached the truck, Julia called on a woman who looked like one of Luis's tías. "What are you going to do for *my* community?" the woman asked. "We have been spat on for years, and we are ready for some dignity."

"I'm glad you asked that question," said Julia Girardo. "What your people have to understand is that handouts are not the answer. Lower taxes that will create jobs. That is what your community needs. . . ." She kept talking. Luis wasn't listening. He was rehearsing what he was going to say. He had to get the words right.

When Julia Girardo paused, he raised his hand.

"Yes!" She pointed and smiled so broadly her cheeks must have hurt. "Isn't that nice? A question from a young person. Go ahead, mijo. What do you want to know?"

"Señora Girardo, I have evidence—," Luis began, but she cut him off.

"Call me Julia. Por favor," she said.

"Julia, I know that you caused the blackout," he said. "I have definite evidence. So my question is, how are you going to pay people back? My parents lost wages for three days of work. Many more people lost money too. Many businesses will have to close down for a while. The news says it will be millions of dollars. Also, Señora, many people have been hurt. How do you pay that back?"

Luis's words took a moment to sink in. When they did, Julia Girardo's smile faded and her face assumed the expression from the crying-baby ad. The quiet lasted long enough that the TV guys, who had been packing up, realized something was going on, something worthy of their viewers' time, and re-aimed their cameras and microphones toward the candidate for mayor.

A particularly enterprising TV reporter beelined for Luis. "Hey, kid, what're you talking about? What do you know?"

At the same time, Tony's guys positioned themselves in a loose ring around the truck. Unless the hunter wanted to run over a kid on live TV, the truck would not drive anywhere soon.

Up till now, Luis had not noticed Nate Bridgewater, but someone must have alerted him that his candidate was in trouble because he hopped up to the truck bed beside her.

"Luis?" He looked into the crowd, his smile as bright as ever. "Is that you, amigo? Julia, never mind that kid. He's my homie. This must be his idea of a joke, but it's not funny."

"No joke," Luis said, aware that three video cameras were now pointed at his face. "It was a cyber crime. The attack surface was the network of ITREX meters in every NJL customer's home or business. Your hacker dropped malware into the server that communicates with the PLC, only maybe you should've paid him more because he made some mistakes with the suicide script. A blind guide dog could've followed the trail he left."

Blind guide dog? Luis thought. *Did I really say that? Did it even make sense?* He hoped he'd said that PLC thing right. He hoped no one asked him if he remembered what it stood for.

"Your driver there," he continued, "he has a hat on now, but I recognize him. He's the bald gentleman who chased me around last night. If anyone's wondering about the fire at 316 Larch Street, he set it. I was there."

This speech was pretty long for Luis, as well as being the first one he had ever made on TV. His heart was pounding, and his voice had gone raspy. He hoped he didn't have to say anything else. Even if he got some of that cyber stuff wrong, it ought to have been enough to convince Uncle Nate and Julia Girardo that he knew what he was talking about, that he knew what they had done.

Then the news guys helped him out. "What's he talking about, Ms. Girardo?" a reporter with a notebook yelled.

"My family's store was *trashed* in the blackout!" said a black woman in the crowd. "You should be ashamed!"

"Pay us back!" somebody cried.

"Pay us back!" said someone else.

Looking shell-shocked, Julia held up her hands for quiet. "My good people," she said. "I don't know this young man, and I can assure you I had *nothing* to do with—"

"I thought it was fishy," Luis heard someone say. "She was out in that truck the moment my lights went out. She was stirring up more trouble."

And then the crowd took up the chant: "Pay us back!"

In the distance, Luis heard a siren.

"You won't rat out my grandpa, will you?" Maura said.

"I got this," Luis said. Then he looked at the angry faces around him, the fear in the eyes of Nate Bridgewater and Julia Girardo, the steely determination of Tony and his guys, the news cameras with eyes unblinking . . . and added, "I think."

Without a backward glance, Uncle Nate swung himself over the tailgate and began walking briskly across the parking lot toward the mall. After a dozen steps, his pace became a jog and then an all-out sprint. Three of Tony's guys gave chase, but Nate Bridgewater was in excellent condition. Seeing his winded, beaten guys turn back, sheepish expressions on their faces, Tony shook his head, disgusted. "That's it. No more cigarettes. And we're cutting down on the fast food too."

Abandoned in the truck bed, Julia backed toward the cab. The hooting crowd was moving forward when three black-and-white Hampton cop cars pulled up. Ordinarily cops were not Luis's favorite people. Today, though, Luis was glad to see them. He didn't want anyone to get hurt because of what he'd said—not even the hunter, not even Julia Girardo.

The officers were out of their cars in a heartbeat, but they didn't know where to turn. The obvious targets were Tony and his gang, but the crowd steered them in another direction, the right direction. The crowd was full of people who had suffered during the blackout, people who wanted someone punished. Julia Girardo was available.

"Stay right where you are, Ms. Girardo," an officer called through his bullhorn. "And you folks, hold your horses now. We are going to get to the bottom of this."

CHAPTER THIRTY

T he police detained both Julia Girardo and her driver—the man Luis had been calling the hunter—without incident. In fact, both of them looked relieved to climb into patrol cars. It probably seemed a whole lot safer than facing an angry crowd.

When the news guys identified Luis as the kid who had asked about the blackout, the police brought him in for questioning. Luis was surprised by how polite the two officers were. One of them he recognized, a Latino guy with silver hair. He was somebody's tío. Luis could not remember whose. The other one was black—taller, thinner, and less sure of himself. Both of them called him "young man" and told him they were impressed with his knowledge of computers and the electric grid.

Luis was kind of impressed with his knowledge too.

He was careful with his answers, though—careful to leave out Maura's grandpa. Instead, he pinned all the glory on Computer Genius, who—according to Luis—had thought of the smart meters on his own.

Where would they find this kid, Computer Genius, the officers wanted to know.

"My house," Luis told them. But when they sent someone to talk to him, Luis's mom said he was gone, vanished back into legend.

"He was here when we returned from Tío Pepe's in Wilmington," Mrs. Cardenal told the officer. "He was very courteous. He asked for a six-pack of Red Bull and three cans of Cheddar Cheese Pringles. I had to go to Cherry Hill to find them. When I came back, he said, 'Gracias, Señora, and adiós.' Then he walked right out the door. I didn't try to stop him. I had plenty else on my mind."

Later the same day, Nordstrom security picked up Nate Bridgewater after a customer reported a suspicious man holed up in a dressing room in women's sportswear. He spent a night in jail before being arraigned along with Julia Girardo on charges including computer fraud, conspiracy to commit computer fraud, use of intercepted communications, and misappropriation of campaign funds.

The evening of the following day—Thursday—Mrs. Girardo, out on bail, called a press conference, apologized to her supporters, and citing changed circumstances, with-drew her candidacy for mayor.

Luis didn't hear this news till Friday morning when he was microwaving oatmeal for breakfast. He was home by himself. His parents, both called back to work, had gone in early to pick up overtime. They had bills to pay—rent, electric-ity, cable, credit cards, groceries. Plus Christmas was coming, and Luis's family always made a big deal out of Christmas.

If Luis had learned one thing from his parents, it was this: Vivir la vida americana cost money. To afford it, you had to work hard.

Luis ate his oatmeal at the kitchen counter, put his bowl in the sink, picked up his phone, and started to text Maura. The news on the radio reminded him there was some stuff he still did not understand.

Then he had a thought and tapped the green phone button. Once in a while, it was easier just to talk.

"How's your grandpa?" Luis said when Maura picked up.

"Not good but better," she said. "Did you hear about Julia Girardo?"

"Yeah, just now, and that's why I'm calling. Can you tell me one thing, Maura? Why did your grandpa wanna help those losers?"

Maura didn't answer right away. In fact, it was so quiet, Luis could hear her breathing. Maybe he shouldn't have asked. But didn't he deserve to know? He had gone to a lot of trouble to protect Mr. O'Hara. He had gone to a lot of trouble period.

Finally, Maura spoke. "I don't know if he'll ever be able to tell me. I don't know if he even knows himself anymore. The stroke messed up his brain. I said something about the blackout yesterday, and he kind of shut down. I have my own idea, though, if you want to hear it."

"Sure, I do," Luis said. "I mean, I guess."

More silence.

"Okay, I definitely want to hear it," Luis said. "Tell me what you think."

Maura took a breath. "So NJL cut my grandpa's pension, the amount he gets paid since he retired. I told you that, right?"

"Either you did, or your mom," Luis said.

"When that happened, my grandpa got mad at the company," Maura said. "He kept saying how he gave the best years of his life to NJL, and they broke their promise, and it wasn't fair. He said the average Joe never gets a break."

"What about the average José?" Luis asked.

"Him too," Maura said. "And Josephine while we're at it."

"Your grandpa might be right," Luis said.

"He might," Maura said. "Anyway, when he talked like that, he sounded like Julia Girardo. You know, big companies and government are out to get the little guy. And she wanted to help the little guy fight back."

"Was she telling the truth about that, do you think?" Luis asked.

"I think she would've said anything to get votes," Maura said. "Anyway, how can you trust a person who would do the damage that she did—the damage she and Uncle Nate did?"

"That question's too big for my brain," Luis said. "But if you're right, I get why your grandpa helped. He was mad at NJL and maybe the world. He knew about smart meters. That made him useful when they decided a black-out would get more people upset, upset enough to vote for someone new for mayor."

"Right," Maura said. "So he lent them a laptop, or gave them the encryption codes. He doesn't remember that now. At least I don't think he does."

Luis thought of something—something bad. "Maura, if we figured this out, maybe the police will. Maybe they'll come for your grandpa."

"I'm afraid of that too," Maura said. "And I'm afraid if they do, it will make him even sicker. But I don't know what to do, hope it doesn't happen, I guess. And hey—I have a question for you."

"Go," Luis said.

"How did you know it was Uncle Nate who sent the text to Grandpa? I'm way smarter than you, and I didn't know."

"Just because you built a fancier science fair project than I did doesn't mean you're—"

"Okay, okay. Sorry. Could you answer the question? Por favor, please?" Maura said.

"I didn't know for sure," Luis admitted, "but you had said that thing about people using birthdays for passcodes. It stuck in my head. And the handle of the guy who texted your grandpa was NB1231."

"NB," Maura repeated. "Nate Bridgewater. And twelve thirty-one . . . that's New Year's Eve. So that's why you asked my mom about his birthday. That was smart, Luis."

"Gracias," said Luis. "I thought of it when you said Nate called your grandpa 'pops.' That word was in the text on your grandpa's phone. And Nate kept interrupting your mom at the hospital. He was afraid I'd see the connection between smart meters and your grandpa."

"He was right to be afraid," Maura said.

"Sí, obviamente," Luis said. "So then he sent Julia Girardo's driver to follow me, see how close I was to solving the mystery, maybe scare me, or worse."

"He did scare you," Maura said. "But I guess that was better than what he did to Tony."

Since school wasn't going to start till Monday, Luis and Maura made a plan to work on their science fair summaries the next day—Saturday. Afterward, Maura could come to Luis's house for ceviche, a Nicaraguan specialty, raw fish marinated in lime juice and hot spices.

"Raw fish?" Maura sounded a little creeped out.

"You'll like it. You'll see," Luis said.

"I'll be polite," Maura said.

"My brother is coming over too," Luis said. "You can invite your mom if you want, and your sister."

"One of them will have to stay with Grandpa," Maura said. "But I'll ask."

"I have one other question," Luis said.

"My brain hurts," Maura said. "But go ahead. What?"

"Do you think I'll win the science fair?" Luis said. "I, uh . . . owe a friend some money."

CHAPTER THIRTY-ONE

Señora Álvaro did not come back from her daughter's house till Saturday. This gave Luis plenty of time to worry about the four hundred and fifty dollars, but nowhere near enough to make a plan to repay it.

Finally, he decided to tell her the truth. Looked at one way, that money bought the power back. The news said the blackout was costing Hampton businesses millions of dollars a day. Compared to that, four hundred and fifty was cheap, right?

On Saturday morning, Luis texted Maura: **Meet me at the bodega. Noon?**

He had decided he needed backup. He was relieved when Maura texted back: **K.**

Señora Álvaro had just turned on the ABIERTO/OPEN sign when Luis rode up on his bike. Maura wasn't there yet, but he went inside. Most of the shelves were still bare, but a delivery guy was unloading a truck outside.

"Buenos días, Luis. Did you bring my box?"

Luis unzipped his backpack, pulled out the box, and handed it over. Señora Álvaro took it without smiling. Luis wished Maura were there. Since the señora would see the IOUs the second she lifted the lid, there was no point putting it off: He explained everything in one long breath.

"You should be proud, Señora," he concluded. "You helped save the city."

Luis had hoped his grand words would impress her.

Or not.

Señora Álvaro nodded but never stopped scowling. "I am happy the loud lady with the truck has been arrested. I am happy we have lights again. And still I want my money. I did not get this far in business by being una buena persona—a good person."

Maura walked in just then. Instead of saying hi, Luis said, "So if you win the science fair, will you share the money? I'll help you with your summary. I promise."

Maura's face flashed surprise, confusion, and annoyance. Luis guessed it might have been a good idea to explain first. Then all at once Maura seemed to figure it out. "Señora Álvaro is the friend you owe money to. That's how you paid Computer Genius."

"Más o menos," Luis said, "more or less."

"Mostly more," said Señora Álvaro.

"I don't need help with my summary," Maura said.

Luis felt stung. Hadn't he brought back the lights? Solved the mystery? Almost gotten burned up in a fire? This being a hero thing was not as good as he expected. In the end it had worked out for Odysseus, but there was a whole lot of cold, wet, bloody, painful misery first. Maybe Odysseus should've stayed home. Maybe he, Luis, should've stayed home too.

"What happened to your face, Luis?" Señora Álvaro asked. "You look like a monster—el chupacabra—"

Luis did not feel like telling her how he got hurt, but Maura did. Was he imagining it, or did Señora Álvaro ease up on her usual scowl? "Maybe we should put on some ointment to help it heal," she said. "There are tubes in one of these boxes. You want to help the tía vieja unpack them? ¿Por favor?"

Luis saw a ray of hope. "Could we maybe repay the loan that way—work it off? There's a lot of boxes to open, stuff to put back on shelves."

"We'll see," said Señora Álvaro. "But for now, apúrense—vámonos. We have work to do."

EPILOGUE

On a Tuesday morning in February, three months after the blackout, four people are sitting in a drab conference room in an equally drab law office in Trenton, New Jersey. One of them is Nate Bridgewater. One of them is his lawyer. The others are lawyers for the plaintiffs: fifty-seven businesses and one individual who want Nate Bridgewater to pay back money lost while the power was out.

This morning, the lawyers are going to record Nate's answers to a whole lot of questions. Nate has decided to tell the truth. Why not? He has almost no money anyway, and very soon he'll be in prison with all expenses paid.

Before the questioning starts, Nate's lawyer reads over the list of plaintiffs—hair salons, auto shops, bodegas, dollar stores, pawn shops, liquor stores, diners. The lone individual is named Peter Joseph.

"What's the deal with this guy?" The lawyer points at the list. "How did he get in here?"

Nate has to think. "Oh, yeah. That must be the kid, the hacker we hired. I probably never paid him. First we were busy with the campaign. After that we were busy getting arrested and thrown in jail."

"Shall we begin?" one of the plaintiffs' lawyers asks.

"Let's do this," says Nate.

The legal proceeding is called a deposition. It's tedious and repetitive. It takes all morning. Finally someone turns off the recorder. Everyone but Nate shuffles papers and returns them to briefcases. One of the plaintiffs' lawyers announces he has a meeting and leaves, but the other one pushes her chair back from the table and looks at Nate. "I have one more question. Off the record."

Nate's lawyer says, "Don't talk to her!"

Nate says, "Oh, go blow your nose. Go ahead, uh—Miss Saunders, am I right? What do you want to know?"

"Why did you pull such a crazy stunt?" Miss Saunders asks.

Nate raises one shoulder and drops it. "It's Politics 101. Scare the people and they'll look for strong leadership. My candidate was the tough guy, the strong man—

even if she did happen to be female. So I manufactured a crisis, scared the people. If you're a campaign manager, it's practically part of the job description."

"But I thought your candidate was leading in the polls?" Miss Saunders says.

"*Was* leading is right. Then that crying baby ad came out, and all of a sudden she was losing. But I had anticipated something might come up. That's why we had the Zap project ready to go. All we had to do was tell the kid to drop the RAT."

Miss Saunders crosses her arms. "There is so much wrong with your reasoning, I hardly know where to start. Think of the damage! Not just to these people but to the city. Don't you feel bad you did what you did?"

Nate thinks about telling this woman to blow her nose, too. She sounds like a Sunday school teacher all of a sudden. But he resists. In prison, he probably won't have a lot of conversations with smart young women.

"Did you perfect that glare in law school?" he asks her. "What I feel bad about is being outsmarted by two nosy kids with time on their hands. For a while, I felt bad about Pops, too, but my guy here assures me he's in the clear. It seems nobody, not even the D.A., wants to go after an old man who just had a stroke."

Nate's lawyer pushes his chair away from the table and stands up, but Miss Saunders isn't done. Wearing a sky-blue jacket and matching headband, she looks younger than she is. "If people can't trust the candidates, can't trust the elections, can't trust their leaders"—she takes a breath—"I don't know. Doesn't democracy fall apart?"

Nate is capable of patience, and he's good at explaining. He thinks maybe he should've have been a teacher. Too late now. "Look, Miss, you seem intelligent, but you've got it exactly backwards. Democracy means government belongs to the people, right? Not me, or you, or Ms. Girardo either. But when something's yours, you're responsible for it. You own it. And when you own something, you're supposed to pay attention to it."

"But honesty—"

"Let me finish," Nate interrupts. "Do the voters study up before they go to the polls? Do they vote for good reasons or because they're scared or they saw somebody frown at a baby? Your average person spends more time choosing toothpaste than choosing a candidate. And as long as that's the way it is, somebody's gonna take advantage. The way I see it, that somebody might as well've been me."

The young lawyer closes her briefcase with a click. Her expression is smug. "Only it didn't work out for you, did it?"

Nate doesn't answer. "You ready to go?" he asks his lawyer.

"I been ready," his lawyer replies.

Nate and Miss Sanders stand up. Nate holds the door for her. She nods curtly and walks out.

"Hey," Nate speaks to her back. "What you said is right. It didn't work out—this time."

"How a Circuit Works"
By Luis Cardenal (edited by Maura Brown)

To understand a circuit, first you've got to understand elec- ,
tricity.

What is electricity? Electrons moving.

What is an electron? A tiny particle in an atom that has a negative charge.

What is a negative charge? It is the opposite of a positive charge. (Not helpful, right?) But particles with negative charges like to hang with particles with positive charges, which are called—surprise!—positrons.

Electricity is nothing but lonely electrons moving through a substance with the goal of meeting up with their friends the positrons.

If we're talking about lightning, the substance is the atmosphere. (That's what Benjamin Franklin showed in his famous kite experiment.)

If we're talking about the electricity in your house, between power poles, or in my circuit, then the substance is metal wire.

A circuit is a loop of something, often copper wire, made for the electrons to follow.

In my project, a battery starts the electrons flowing at the negative terminal and gives them a place to go, the positive terminal. On the way, they move through the bulb, causing the filament inside it to glow.

The electrons move only if they have a clear path to their hearts' desire, the positrons. In other words, they move only if there is no break in the circuit. When the switch is off, it breaks that circuit and the electrons come to a halt so that the filament stops glowing—the light goes dark. When the switch is on, the circuit is complete and the electrons get going, turning on the light.

A NOTE TO THE READER

Dear Reader,

Growing up in Camden, New Jersey, I never thought any-one would want to write a book based on me.

But that's exactly what *Zap!* is—a book based on me as a kid.

Of course, the author did change a few details—like my last name and the name of my hometown. Also, I never actually had to play detective in the case of a massive power outage the way Luis and Maura do in the story.

But the author, who is my good friend, kept the important stuff—like what it's like to be the American son of immigrants from Nicaragua growing up in a city that's seen more prosperous times. In the story, Luis hangs out in abandoned houses, relies on his big brother, sees gang violence firsthand, has a lot of tías and tíos who are not blood relatives, fears the police, relies on the neigh-borhood bodega for groceries, is a fan of *The Odyssey*, and sometimes has trouble communicating with his very hard-working parents.

All those things were true for me too.

Also like Luis in the book, I realized early that I had a

choice. I could blow off school, have a good time on the streets, and become another statistic. That was the path of some friends, family members, and neighbors, the ones less lucky than me. Some I never heard from after we grew up, and some are in jail. The alternative was to work hard the way my teachers and my siblings wanted me to. That meant having faith in myself even when other people did not.

I can't say I didn't make mistakes. I got into trouble sometimes as a teenager, and I did some stupid, dangerous things. But I worked hard in high school to earn good grades. Getting involved in cross country and lacrosse helped me blow off steam. My efforts were repaid when I was able to enroll at a good university to study civil engineering. After graduating in 2010, I found a nice job but soon realized I had a greater calling: I wanted to serve my country. In the navy, I shipped out for active duty to help the construction effort in the Kandahar province in Afghanistan.

My job there was to help coordinate deconstruction of a U.S. base while at the same time supporting the construction capabilities of the Afghan National Army.

I had always thought of myself as a pretty self-disciplined person, and my time in the military reinforced that. Sailors worked under me, so I also had to learn how to lead. Some people might tell you that the culture of Afghanistan is different from America's, but I felt a strong connection to the people there. Like me growing up, they knew what it was to face violence. They didn't have much in the way of material wealth. To get by, they relied on family and friends as well as their own inner strength. They were tough because they had to be.

Today I am back in the States working in the profession I studied for in college, transportation engineering, which means I help cities and towns improve roads and build new ones. Most of the time it's a fun job. Digging around in old records to find out where water, gas, and electric lines were laid decades ago is a little like treasure hunting. Figuring out the best way to accommodate old structures while building new ones is like solving a puzzle.

I have lived in several U.S. cities and towns but now am back in Camden, where I recently bought a house. When I'm not working, I run long distances and bike, besides volunteering for Team RWB, which supports veterans. I have also established a local chapter of Students Run for kids ages twelve to eighteen. We meet multiple times a week after school to train for distance races.

With running, the accomplishments are measurable: Work hard, and you will see your distances and speeds improve. Maybe because I am a numbers kind of person, seeing my own improvement over the years has been a source of pride. I hope to impart my experience and knowledge to a new generation of urban youth.

I wasn't sure what to think when my friend Martha told me she wanted to put me in a book. Then she said she thought there should be more stories about kids like me, and I agreed. In fact, I wish I had had a book like this when I was a kid, a book about a bona fide hero who also happened to be tough and Latino, a book about a kid who wants to understand the way things work.

My experience and my observations have taught me that no one's upbringing guarantees their future, either for better or worse. Good people can come from anywhere. In my hometown of Camden today there are a lot of good people doing a lot of good things.

Sincerely,
Luis Gaitan

Luis Gaitan all dressed up at age twelve for his baptism, pictured with his mother, Esperanza Gonzalez.

Luis Gaitan at age nine or ten on the Jersey Shore.

Luis Gaitan in his naval uniform, pictured with both parents, Carlos Gaitan and Esperanza Gonzalez, in 2017.

ACKNOWLEDGMENTS

The idea for a book about the power grid came from my always inspirational friend, Anthony LoCicero, to whom *Zap!* is dedicated. Anthony's colleague, Robert B. Swayne, chief electrical engineer at Burns Engineering, is an authority on the grid who helped me get started by telling me about the Conowingo plant over lunch, then went on to review and correct the manuscript. I am also indebted to:

Computer analyst and programmer Suzanne White for help with the hacking and computing details;

Both Emma Paras, emergency preparedness planner at the Children's Hospital of Philadelphia, and Samantha Phillips, director of the National Center for Security and Preparedness at the State University of New York, Albany, for help with all things emergency management;

The well-educated (and fast!) Alejandra Margueytio who reviewed the Spanish;

Stephen Peluso, Ph.D., research associate in mechanical engineering, Penn State University, who—as usual—reviewed everything and made many helpful suggestions, besides noticing that the model number of the fictional

ACKNOWLEDGMENTS

Itron smart meter coincides with the pi sequence following 3.14159.

The real Luis—Luis Gaitan—who generously slows down enough to run with me sometimes.

Finally, thanks to my always astute editor Sylvie Frank for her enduring tough love, and to my publisher, Paula Wiseman, who continues to believe in the importance of bringing STEM concepts to life.

LUIS HAD QUESTIONS
HERE ARE SOME ANSWERS

Luis likes to know how things work, and in the course of the story he asks a lot of questions. Mrs. Brown and Maura answer some of them. Here are some additional answers.

How does a crank radio work?

To understand the crank radio, you have to understand generators. Some of this is explained earlier, but here is a bit more detail.

In 1831 an Englishman named Michael Faraday found that he could produce a steady electric current by spinning a coil of wire around a magnet. In other words, the magnetic force excited the electrons in the wire, and they began to move from one atom to another. This principle, called electromagnetic induction, changes mechanical energy—spinning—into electrical energy. (An electric *motor* does the opposite—changes electrical energy into mechanical energy.)

The spinning turbines that provide electricity today work on the principle Faraday figured out. Some are spun by falling water, some by wind, some by steam created from burning coal, oil, or a nuclear reaction, and some by the exhaust of burning natural gas.

A crank radio like the one Maura's grandfather has tucked away for emergencies uses this principle too. Turning the crank using muscle power spins the wire, generating electric current. It's not necessary to turn the crank at a perfectly constant rate because a regulator makes sure the voltage—the force pushing electrons through the wire—doesn't vary enough to damage the radio. Some crank radios have batteries inside that are charged by the action of the crank.

You might be thinking that if cranking can make a radio work, human power—say pedaling a stationary bike—might be enough to power your house. Unfortunately—not yet. Current technology isn't efficient enough to make this possible. The average American household uses about 1,250 watt-hours (1.25 kilowatt-hours) of energy every hour, while pedaling a bike hooked up to a generator produces only about 110 watt-hours (0.11 kilowatt-hours) every hour. You and eleven or twelve friends would have to do nothing but pedal full-time to keep the household going.

How do solar cells produce electricity?

Light contains energy. When sunlight hits your skin, the energy turns into heat. But not all materials behave like skin. Some are photovoltaic, which means they turn light energy into electricity instead of into heat. One photovoltaic material is a metalloid called silicon. When light hits a silicon crystal, the electrons in it become excited, break their chemical bonds, and jump from one place to another.

Sound familiar?

That's an electric current!

This is a nifty, simple way to make electricity, and there is no shortage of sunlight. Two things make their use problematic. First, there is no good way to regulate the amount of energy a photovoltaic cell produces once it's installed. Second—as Mrs. Brown explains in the book—even with the latest technology, it is difficult to store large amounts of electrical energy. Ironically, if a photovoltaic plant were producing a lot of energy on a sunny day, other power plants would have to be turned down to ensure that supply aligned with demand.

How does nuclear power work?

Luis thinks it would be cool if the electricity that comes from nuclear power were radioactive. Actually, it wouldn't be cool. It would be dangerous! While controlled radioactivity is used by doctors to diagnose and treat health problems, uncontrolled radioactivity produces rays that harm living cells and cause disease, including cancer.

Nuclear power plants work the same way other power plants do. They use steam to power turbines. The difference is this: The heat that boils the water comes from nuclear fission.

What's nuclear fission?

As you've already learned, atoms contain electrons and protons. Uranium atoms are large—they contain ninety-two of each, and the force holding them together is weaker than it is in smaller atoms. Nuclear fission is what happens when you zap a uranium atom with a neutron (an atomic particle with no electric charge), and the atom splits apart. The split generates heat, which is used to boil water in a nuclear power plant.

Atomic bombs also rely on nuclear fission.

Each time an atom splits, more neutrons shoot away, and those neutrons split more atoms, which shoot more neutrons, and so on. If it isn't stopped, this chain reaction will soon generate an explosive amount of heat as well as harmful radioactive rays.

In a power plant, metal control rods absorb the neutrons and stop the chain reaction before an explosion happens.

What is AC power?

AC stands for alternating current. DC stands for direct current. AC current cycles—reverses direction—many times per second, a measurement known as hertz (Hz). North American electric grids typically use AC power that reverses direction sixty times per second, so it cycles at sixty hertz.

Traditionally, the main advantage of AC power over DC is that it can be transformed more easily to higher voltages for long-distance travel over powerlines, and to lower voltages for delivery to customers like houses and businesses.

In the 1880s, the immigrant inventor Nikola Tesla developed AC motors and transformers in the United States. Later, he sold his patents to the industrialist George Westinghouse, who helped establish the power grid that still exists.

These days, DC power has become increasingly prevalent for long-distance transmission, and most experts believe a grid using both systems is best.

What is the power grid?

The power grid is the network of power lines and transformers that distributes electricity from generating plants to users. Luis makes a good guess about the power grid when he compares it to a grid drawn on graph paper. Like that, it's all interconnected. You might look at it as the largest machine ever built.

The grid is not perfect. In fact, it has two big problems. First, because so much of it is outdoors, it can be damaged both by wildlife and weather. Second, it loses energy in the process of generation and in the process of distribution, making it less than optimally efficient.

One way to improve efficiency and save energy is to

make the grid smarter, that is, to automate sensors, computing, and communications to make generation and distribution of electricity respond more quickly to users' needs.

The digital electric meters mentioned in the story are part of that smart grid. Today the U.S. Department of Energy, utility companies, industry groups, and manufacturers recognize the potential for cyberattack and do their best to ensure that smart meters and the system as a whole are protected. The science and engineering in *Zap!* is real, but in the real world, bad guys could not so easily cause a blackout.

In other words, readers, don't try this at home.

Were there tall buildings before elevators?

Yes. The Grand Pyramid at Giza is almost five hundred feet tall (fifty stories), and it was built more than 4,500 years ago. Many European cathedrals, built hundreds of years ago, are four hundred to five hundred feet tall as well.

However, no one had to carry groceries up the stairs of either pyramids or churches. The development of the first tall buildings in which people lived and worked did coincide with the first skyscraper. This did not happen until Elisha Graves Otis's most important invention, an elevator safe enough for passengers, debuted at the 1854 World's Fair in New York City.

Otis's first elevators, which had a brake to prevent a fall in the event a cable broke, were powered by steam. Later in the century, electric motors—much more practical—were added.

An early residential building to take advantage of the new technology was the ten-story Dakota on Central Park West in New York City, which still stands. Built for the well-to-do in 1882, the Dakota had its own electric generating plant to power lights and the elevator.

ASSEMBLING YOUR OWN EMERGENCY KIT

Mr. O'Hara had a closet full of supplies ready in case of an emergency like a power outage. The Red Cross and the Federal Emergency Management Agency (FEMA) have suggestions online for what to include in your own, or you can buy one ready-made from a number of sources. Most provide a three-day supply.

Here are some things you will want to include:

- A gallon of water per day per person for drinking and cleaning. For three days, that's three gallons per person.
- Nonperishable food—canned or prepackaged—and a can opener.
- Battery-powered radio (or a hand-crank radio like the one in the book) and spare batteries.
- Flashlights and lanterns, headlamp, extra batteries.
- Moist towelettes (baby wipes) for cleaning.
- First aid kit with Band-Aids, prescription medications, antibiotic spray or cream, analgesic such as aspirin or ibuprofen.

- Wrench to turn off utilities.
- Extra cell phone and/or computer batteries.
- Blankets.
- A cooler for frozen and refrigerated foods.

BIBLIOGRAPHY

Koppel, Ted. *Lights Out: A Cyberattack, a Nation Unprepared, Surviving the Aftermath*. New York: Penguin Random House, 2015.

Schewe, Phillip. *The Grid: A Journey through the Heart of Our Electrified World*. Washington, DC: Joseph Henry Press, 2007.

Survive the Blackout, a website for National Geographic Channel's *American Blackout*, accessed September 28, 2017, http://www.survivetheblackout.com.

Zetter, Kim. *Countdown to Zero Day: Stuxnet and the Launch of the World's First Digital Weapon*. New York: Broadway Books, 2014.

On hacking

Naone, Erica. "Hacking the Smart Grid." *MIT Technology Review*, August 2, 2010, https://www.technologyreview.com/s/420061/hacking-the-smart-grid/.

Sink, Justin. "Russian Hacking Code Found in Vermont Power Utility Computer." *Bloomberg*, December 31, 2016, http://www.bloomberg.com/news/articles/2016-12-31/russian-hacking-code-found-in-vermont-power-utility-computer.

Zetter, Kim. "The Sony Hackers Were Causing Mayhem Years Before They Hit the Company." *Wired*, February 24, 2016, https://www.wired.com/2016/02/sony-hackers-causing-mayhem-years-hit-company/.

On electricity

Brain, Marshall; William Harris; and Robert Lamb. "How Electricity Works." *How Stuff Works*. Accessed September 28, 2017, http://science.howstuffworks.com/electricity.htm.

Edison Tech Center. "Basics of Electricity." Accessed September 28, 2017, http://www.edisontechcenter.org/basics.html.

HyperPhysics, a website hosted by the Department of Physics and Astronomy at Georgia State University. Accessed September 28, 2017, http://hyperphysics.phy-astr.gsu.edu/hbase/magnetic/motorac.html#c2.

The Physics Classroom. "Lesson 1: Electric Potential." Accessed September 28, 2017, http://www.physicsclassroom.com/class/circuits/Lesson-1/Electric-Potential.

Woodford, Chris. "Power Plants." *Explain That Stuff*. Accessed September 28, 2017, http://www.explainthatstuff.com/powerplants.html.

GLOSSARY OF SPANISH WORDS AND PHRASES

abierto: open

abuela: grandmother

apúrense: hurry

aquí: here

¡Ay, qué lástima!: Oh, what a shame!

bodega: convenience store

buena persona: good person

buena suerte con el desayuno: good luck with breakfast

buenas noches: good night

bueno: good

buenos días: good morning

cerrado: closed

el chupacabra: literally means "goat sucker"; a mythical monster from Central and South America

dígame: tell me (formal)

Dios mío: oh my God

¿Entiendes?: Do you understand?

espero que sea muy pronto: I hope that will be very soon

¿Estás aquí?: Are you here?

guácala: gross

hasta luego: see you later

hola: hello

hue: (pronounced "way") slang meaning "man" or "dude"

imbécil: imbecile; stupid

¡Levántate!: Get up! (a command)

me tengo que ir: gotta go

muchísimas gracias: thank you very much

necesito ayuda: I need help

no comiences: a command meaning "don't start," as in
   "don't start with me"

obviamente: obviously

pero lo más importante: but the most important thing

por favor: please

¿Por qué no?: Why not?

por supuesto: of course

puedes probarlo: you can give it a try

¿Qué quieres?: What do you want?

¿Quién sabe?: Who knows?

quizás: maybe; perhaps

Señor / Señora: Mister / Missus

sí: yes

sin papeles: literally "without papers"; refers to undocumented immigrants

tal vez: maybe

tíos / tías: uncles / aunts

todo el tiempo: all the time

tontos: fools

tú siempre molestas: you're always bothering (me)

¿Tuviste suerte?: Did you have any luck?

un momentito: just a minute

vamos: let's go

vivir la vida americana: living life the American way